COWBOY BAD BOYS

Shackled by the Cowboy Drifter
Branded by the Texas Rancher
Bound by the Montana Mountain Man

Jan Bowles

EROTIC ROMANCE

Siren Publishing, Inc.
www.SirenPublishing.com

A SIREN PUBLISHING BOOK
IMPRINT: Erotic Romance

COWBOY BAD BOYS
Shackled by the Cowboy Drifter
Branded by the Texas Rancher
Bound by the Montana Mountain Man
Copyright © 2011 by Jan Bowles

ISBN-10: 1-61034-275-5
ISBN-13: 978-1-61034-275-9

First Printing: March 2011

Cover design by Jinger Heaston
All cover art and logo copyright © 2011 by Siren Publishing, Inc.

ALL RIGHTS RESERVED: This literary work may not be reproduced or transmitted in any form or by any means, including electronic or photographic reproduction, in whole or in part, without express written permission.

All characters and events in this book are fictitious. Any resemblance to actual persons living or dead is strictly coincidental.

Printed in the U.S.A.

PUBLISHER
Siren Publishing, Inc.
www.SirenPublishing.com

DEDICATION

For my Mother Iris May Beazley Lloyd
Born 1st February 1931 - Died Christmas Day 2010
Until we meet again, may God bless you my darling.

"Do not stand at my grave and weep;
I am not there. I do not sleep.
I am a thousand winds that blow.
I am the diamond glints on snow.
I am the sunlight on ripened grain.
I am the gentle autumn rain.
When you awaken in the morning's hush
I am the swift uplifting rush
Of quiet birds in circled flight.
I am the soft stars that shine at night.
Do not stand at my grave and cry;
I am not there. I did not die."
ANON

SIREN PUBLISHING *Classic*

JAN BOWLES

Cowboy Bad Boys

SHACKLED BY THE COWBOY DRIFTER

SHACKLED BY THE COWBOY DRIFTER

Cowboy Bad Boys 1

JAN BOWLES
Copyright © 2011

Chapter One

Zack tensed his muscles. Something didn't feel right. Those footsteps had been following him down this dark street for a few minutes now, and they were getting too close. Just as he was about to turn around and confront whomever it was, he felt a rush of air. A heavy blow smashed across his temple. He crashed to the ground, the left side of his face making painful contact with the pavement.

With barely a moment to think, a crushing pain slammed into his ribs and he doubled up. He reached inside his jacket and pulled out the Smith and Wesson. In some discomfort he hissed through clenched teeth. "You can stop right there, *amigo*." Luckily his breath began to fill his lungs once more. He edged to a nearby wall and braced his back against it.

He eyed the dark, swarthy man warily. Caught in the process of stealing his bag, his assailant stood frozen to the spot, like some cartoon character with one arm reaching forward.

When Zack wiped his free hand across his mouth, blood stained his fingers. Yep, this asshole had damn near caved the one side of his face in.

Waving the gun at his attacker, he spoke again, "Now, we can either do this the hard way, or the easy way. Just back off and get the fuck out of here before I change my mind."

His swarthy nemesis appeared to contemplate the situation. Beads of sweat dripped down his face as he looked first at Zack and then the bag.

"Like I said, I don't care if I have to blow your fucking brains out. You're not the first, and you won't be the last." Zack eased himself into a standing position. Thankfully, his ribs didn't feel broken. "What's it to be?" He'd reached the end of the line. It would all be over if he let him get away with it.

The man smiled. "*Adios, amigo.*" Slowly he retreated, holding his hands in full view. Eventually, when he'd reached far enough away, he turned and disappeared quickly down a side alley.

Zack stuffed the Smith and Wesson back into the waistband of his jeans. He'd been right to bring it with him. Tijuana was full of bandits. Reaching down, he scooped up his hat, dusted it down, and picked up his bag.

He caught his reflection in the shop window. Blood oozed down his cheek, and he wiped it away with the back of his hand. He hardly recognized himself anymore. Just when had he become such a mercenary bastard? Deep down he knew the exact moment he'd changed. His life had simply been blown away. Now all that remained was a hardened, empty shell.

Even Renee wouldn't know him now. He remembered the last words he'd spoken to her. *"Don't worry, baby, everything will be fine. Just trust me."* Unfortunately, life didn't always work out so perfectly. As bitterness consumed him once more, he turned away in disgust at his reflection.

* * * *

Ash watched the tall cowboy enter the diner where she worked. Dressed in jeans, a white shirt, and a tan leather waistcoat, he found a seat and looked around for a waitress to take his order. He was too far away to see clearly, but she could already tell he had a great physique. The man could move mountains with those muscles. He removed his hat and placed it on the seat next to him then pulled a menu from the stand. As he was on one of her tables, she looked forward to getting a closer view.

Finally, she finished taking the order from a particularly obnoxious family. Their two children just wouldn't sit still. They'd made faces at her from the moment they'd walked in.

After placing the order with Ron on the grill, she turned to Maisy, a waitress on another station. "I swear it, if they don't start treating me with a little respect soon, I'll drop the ice cream they've ordered straight into their laps."

Her friend chuckled. "Now don't let them get to you, darlin'. You need to concentrate on the dish that just settled into table five. I'd drop ice cream into his lap anytime, and I'd lick it off him for free."

Ash giggled. "Me, too. Only I'd pay to do it."

Maisy raised her eyebrows. "You've been single for far too long, girl."

Ron leaned across the counter. "Are you girls gonna stop gossiping and do some work?"

"Don't make out like you're hard done by, Ron. I know you just love all the juicy gossip."

"You bet. It brightens my day listening to you two." He slapped four burgers on the grill, and they sizzled loudly.

Taking no notice of Ron, Maisy motioned to Ash with her hand. "Shoo. What are you waiting for? Go take his order. I'll serve the *The Munster Family* for you."

With pad and pencil ready, Ash walked up to table five. He was still studying the menu, so she let her gaze wander from the tip of his cowboy boots, past the tight fitting Wranglers, to his strong muscular chest.

This guy did some serious workouts. She could clearly see the six-pack abs under his tight-fitting clothes.

Girl, you need to get a grip and stop salivating.

Maisy was right. She'd been without a man for far too long. Nine months seemed an awful long time to be single, but then hadn't she been burned badly by Rob? She hadn't looked at another man since they'd split. Well, not until now.

Ash noted his black, wavy collar-length hair that fell about his temples, the strong jaw line, the way his large hands held on firmly to the menu. His skin the color of warm teak appeared rugged and weather-beaten. He looked to be in his mid-thirties. When his eyes finally locked with hers, she swallowed hard. Bright blue and striking against his well-tanned skin, they simply took her breath away.

"What can I get you, cowboy?" Her voice sounded shaky even to her own ears, and she hoped he didn't notice.

"I'll have ham, with eggs over easy." She assumed from his drawl he was from the South. So he wasn't a local. Too bad, the guy was just probably passing through.

"Say, do you have any grits?"

She shook her head, pointing with her pencil. "Only what's on the menu."

"Hmm, then I'll have hash browns and coffee."

He nodded as she repeated his order back to him. He seemed to notice her for the first time, his gaze slowly travelling from her hands to her face. She had a sudden feeling that he'd ripped the clothes right off her.

"Is that an English accent?"

"Yes," she answered. Now that he'd turned toward her, she noticed the cuts on the one side of his face. The man looked dangerous, and just a little exciting.

"Don't tell me. You came to seek your fame and fortune in Hollywood but ended up waiting tables instead." With an amused expression on his face, he leaned back in his seat and waited for her to answer.

If she hadn't been so annoyed by his glib observation, her jaw would have dropped open. He had her life story to a T in just five minutes flat. She gave him a tight smile. "Yes, we're a sad bunch. Like the song said, 'All the stars that never were, are pumping gas and parking cars.' Guess you now know why I work in this sleazy diner, serving dumbass customers."

Before he could say anything, she lifted up her notepad and continued, "I'd better place your order, cowboy." With that, she turned and walked away.

* * * *

Zack chuckled to himself as the waitress went to take an order from another table. She sure had bristled at his personal remarks. He could tell them a mile off. The perfect white smile. A toned body to die for. With her chestnut-highlighted hair all cascading onto her shoulders and her perfect manicure, it hadn't taken him long to work it out.

She'd certainly piqued his curiosity with her refined English accent. The little pocket rocket couldn't be more than five-foot-three. Very attractive and petite, her large, green eyes had stared him down.

He shook his head and focused back on more pressing needs. Business had demanded that he leave Mexico in a hurry, so he hadn't slept for two days. He'd rest this afternoon and then write up his report tomorrow. He checked his watch just as Little Miss Perfect brought his coffee to the table.

"Is it so obvious that I look like an out-of-work actress?" she asked.

He shrugged as his gaze wandered over her. Typically, she wore far too much makeup. "Aspiring actresses have this fake look about them."

Her eyes narrowed on him, and her mouth firmed into a thin line. "Perhaps you should revise that comment, cowboy," she stated sarcastically.

"What I mean is, they look manufactured and over-the-top." Hell, now he'd gone and said something far worse. See where losing sleep had got him? Thank God she wasn't out to kill him. "I'll rephrase that—"

"Mister, perhaps you should just quit while you're ahead."

He nodded, his gaze coming to rest on the name badge pinned to her chest. "I think you should just forget that I said anything—Ashley."

Without looking at him, she answered, "Don't worry, cowboy, I already have." Spinning quickly on her heels, she walked away. Now that didn't happen very often. A haughty English woman had really put him in his place.

Chapter Two

Ash ordered a white wine and settled into an empty booth. The bar was dimly lit, and she eased back into the seat. She didn't usually drink alone, but she'd had one hell of a day. Plagued by stupid customers and a disastrous casting for a bit part, she needed a pick me up. A glass of Chardonnay would certainly hit the spot.

The small condo where she lived in Long Beach, California, had grated on her nerves ever since she'd arrived home. So she'd showered, put on a red, backless dress, and headed across the road to The Hub, a small, friendly dance bar. She knew some of the people there, so she didn't feel too conspicuous.

Within a half-hour, she'd begun to relax. Every now and then, a couple would head onto the dance floor to make out. Now that was something she missed, the close contact with a man. She guessed it was her own fault that she was still single. She'd been asked out quite a few times since Rob had left the scene, but at the time she'd been reluctant to start another relationship. She just didn't want to get hurt again.

Chuck the barman came over to her table and placed a drink in front of her.

"What's that for?" she asked.

He pointed behind her. "Guy at the bar bought it for you. Said it's by way of an apology."

Ash craned her head. The asshole cowboy from the diner raised his bottle of Bud. As her eyes locked on his, he smiled. The guy had seriously pissed her off, and yet here she was smiling back at him. What was wrong with her?

Well, that smile had done it. Wearing jeans and a black T-shirt, the cowboy sauntered over to her table. He appeared even more muscular and tall up close. As he stood over her, she guessed about six-three and two hundred pounds. His dark, disheveled hair fell about his face, giving him a devilish appearance.

Watch out Ashley, this guy may just roast you alive.

"Mind if I join you?"

"Do I have a choice?" With her heart in her mouth, she watched as he settled his athletic frame into the seat opposite. His piercing blue eyes rested on her as he leaned back against the velour upholstery. He pointed to her glass of wine. "Peace offering."

"What for?"

"I'm afraid I acted out of character in the diner. I'm not normally such an asshole."

"You could have fooled me."

He smiled. His wicked grin sent goose bumps down her spine. His eyes showed amusement and twinkled from the surrounding lights as he stared at her. "I hadn't slept for two days. Though that's still no excuse."

"No, it isn't."

"Then allow me to apologize once more, Ashley."

With his dark locks falling about his temples, and a smile on his lips, she felt rooted to the spot. The word predatory came to mind, and she reminded herself that she could very easily become his prey. "Very well. Apology accepted, Mister...?"

"Zack Delaney, but please call me Zack." He held out his hand. "Nice to meet you, Ashley."

"Ashley Carmicheal, but you can call me Ash. I've always preferred the shorter version of my name."

He reached across and took her hand in his, squeezing it lightly. His flesh felt warm to the touch, and a tingling sensation surged through her veins. She felt vulnerable just being in his presence. His gaze finally came to lock with hers. Startling blue, his eyes held her entranced until she said, "Thanks for the wine, Zack. I don't normally drink alone, but I had one hell of a day. I just couldn't stomach the close confines of my apartment anymore."

"Yeah, bit like the four walls of my motel room."

His rich southern drawl gave him a tough, masculine edge. He had a certain ruthless quality to him. He'd already aroused her interest more than she cared to admit. She stared at him. Once more she noticed the cuts and grazes on his cheek. "So what happened to your face?"

"Some local difficulty in Tijuana."

"Hmm, you should be more careful." With his face all grazed, he looked like six-feet three-inches of pure trouble. He appeared dangerous and out of control. He was everything that she knew she should avoid, but he excited her, too. Simply put, he turned her on.

"So what part of England are you from, Ash?"

"Cheltenham. You've probably never heard of it."

"I have, actually. Horse racing, I believe."

"That's it." As she spoke with him, she realized how desperately lonely she'd become. Why hadn't she noticed before? That's why she added, "I miss home. I've decided to give the acting up on my next birthday. I'll be thirty next year. I guess I've been holding back, thinking my family will see me as a failure."

"I doubt it. Most people never get to follow their dreams."

"Yes, well, my dreams only make me sad at the moment. I completely fluffed a casting audition I had this morning. I auditioned for the role of a hooker."

"Hence the heavy makeup this morning."

Ash giggled. "Precisely, Zack. Everything is not always as it seems in Tinseltown."

"So, how come you're all on your own tonight, Ash? Is there someone else?"

It had been a long time since she'd played this game. She'd been out of the market for nearly ten years. She shook her head and let her fingers drift over her wineglass. "I guess I'm still nursing the after-effects of a nasty split. I'm afraid I got really hurt, so I've deliberately kept to myself."

"That's too bad."

She nodded. "How about you? Are you married?" As soon as she uttered the words, she wished she could withdraw them. What did it matter, she was hardly going to see him again. He looked surprised that she'd even asked, so she added, "Surely you are, you must be in your thirties."

He grinned at her. "I'm thirty-five, and I was married for a time."

"But you're not anymore?"

He stared at her for a moment and then shook his head. "No, not anymore." Ash wondered if the relief she felt was evident on her face. The fact that he appeared unattached had momentarily made her heart rate increase.

"So, cowboy, you're not from these parts. Where are you from?"

"Lived in Louisiana for a time," he drawled. "I haven't lived there for a while, though. When Katrina struck, it clear blew my life away."

"Were you there when it happened?"

"Sure was. The scariest moment of my life, too." He looked thoughtful for a moment as he reflected on the event. It was just enough for her to realize he'd lost a lot. A deep sadness tinged his eyes, and she wanted to know more.

"What happened?"

"Like I said, I lost everything." His steely gaze rested on her, and she knew not to probe further. Whatever it was, he didn't like talking about it.

"So what have you been doing since?"

"You know how it is. Lives drift, don't they? Plus, I had a few problems I had to deal with. I've been in Mexico for the last few years." He studied her for a moment. His gaze lingered on hers and then focused on her mouth. Then he looked briefly away as he cleared his throat and said, "Say, Ash, would you like to dance?"

The thought of dancing with him, up close and personal, made her blush, and she shook her head, forcing a giggle from her lips to hide her nervousness. "I'm sure I've forgotten how to dance. I'd just make a fool of myself."

"Somehow I don't think you would, but you can't knock a guy for asking. How about I get us both another drink? Maybe you'll say yes when I ask you again."

She smiled. "So you don't take no for an answer then?"

"Nope." His eyes flickered briefly across her face.

She watched him slide from the booth and walk over to the bar. He rested one booted foot on the brass rail and leaned against the oak counter. Confidence oozed from every pore in his body. The muscles in his arms tensed and flexed as he reached into his back jean pocket and removed his wallet. She could just envisage those strong arms wrapped around her, holding her tight. They promised her the world, if only for one night. Her eyes closed as the thought enveloped her. She saw exactly where this evening was leading, and she had no intention of running for the hills. Maybe just for tonight, she wouldn't feel quite so lonely.

"Thank you," she said as he returned with another round of drinks. She leaned on her elbow and smiled at him. "So where do you call home?"

"I have a house near Bogalusa, Louisiana. It's been rebuilt, but up to now I haven't wanted to return."

"Why?"

"Too many memories, I guess. I'm in the process of selling it at the moment. I want to buy a ranch up in Montana."

"Why Montana?"

"I've been there a few times. I don't know. I liked it. Seems a good place to settle down and stop drifting."

She sensed his deep sadness again, pervading his every thought. "Well, I hope you find what you're looking for."

"Me too," he said gruffly. He raised the bottle to his lips and looked at her. "Now how about that dance?"

"Okay, but I warn you, I'm rusty."

"There's nothing to it. You'll be fine, just lean on me."

Now that's what she was afraid of. As soon as he led her onto the dance floor, she became aware of every last inch of him. One of his strong hands grasped hers and the other clasped firmly around her waist. She couldn't help but shiver as his fingers grazed across the bare flesh of her back.

Wearing high stilettos, she just reached his broad shoulder. His heady, masculine scent overwhelmed her as the heat from his body permeated the thin material of her dress.

His well-defined lips smiled at her. "See, not so rusty, are we?"

Ash began to drift as he pulled her closer, lost in the warmth of his embrace.

Chapter Three

Frankly, asking Ash to dance had been Zack's way of stopping the memories surfacing. After some persuasion, he'd eventually managed to coax her onto the dance floor. He hadn't planned any of this, but she looked as lonely as he felt.

When he'd first spotted her in the bar, he'd sent over a glass of wine, thinking that would be that. A peace offering if you like, but when she'd smiled at him, he'd thought what the fuck. He had to admit, he'd been rather rude to her in the diner. Just why he didn't know. He could only put it down to the fact that he'd been around low life for far too long, and because he hadn't slept for nearly two days, his manners had deserted him, big time. Most people deserved his respect, and it would be wise to remember that.

He glanced down. It had been a long time since he'd held a woman like this in his arms, let alone danced with one. When his life had been destroyed, he just hadn't wanted to continue, never mind date someone. Of course he'd had women, but not the sort you'd want to get to know afterwards. Yet this petite English woman had made an impact on him already. Too bad he'd be moving on tomorrow.

Her green eyes were so close now as they connected with his, he could see the flecks of gold that fanned around the irises. They were eyes he could lose himself in, if only for a few hours.

When his hand caressed the bare skin of her back, he felt her body shiver as she responded to his touch. He felt satisfaction run through his veins knowing that she was attracted to him. His cock hardened uncomfortably in his tight jeans at the thought of her lying beneath him, all naked and hot for him.

Yeah, the evening had started to get a whole lot more interesting.

He pulled her closer so that she would feel the hard length of his cock against her belly. He guessed if she wasn't interested, she'd soon tell him where to go. Instead of pulling away, she pressed herself closer, moving her hand to the nape of his neck and teasing her fingers through his hair.

She smelt of summer meadows, and he closed his eyes and savored the moment. What was wrong with two lonely people needing each other, if only for a little while?

The music eddied and flowed around them, and several records later, he spoke her name, "Ash."

"Hmm?"

"Let's get the hell out of here."

* * * *

As soon as they walked outside, he pulled her into his arms and pressed her hard against the wall. His lips sought hers, persuasive and demanding. Her breath shortened as his knee pressed between her legs and anchored her fast.

Zack handled her with an ownership that she found exhilarating.

"Now, how about we explore this mutual attraction somewhere a little more private? My motel room is just a ten-minute walk away."

Trapped where she stood, his heat enveloped her. Before she could answer, his mouth captured hers with an infinite satisfaction, his tongue delving and tousling with hers. Already aroused by the intimate contact of dancing together in the bar for the last hour, her panties dampened even more. His hand rubbed possessively into the juncture of her thighs, grazing her clit with worldly experience.

There would be no fumbling around, just a man giving her exactly what she needed, hot, pleasurable, mind blowing sex.

Breaking the kiss, she breathlessly answered, "I only live across the road."

He smiled. "Even better."

For what seemed a long time, she just stared at him through her lashes. Plain dangerous came to mind. Surely she should run a mile. Yet the thrill seeker within her ignored her misgivings, and she finally motioned toward her condo.

Anticipation flooded her mind as they walked the short distance across the road. He was tall and broad, and God help her, powerful. She swallowed hard. Tonight, he was exactly what she needed.

Her apartment was on the first floor and had been her home for the past few months. It felt warm and inviting when she opened the door. The open-plan living area had her familiar possessions. Two over-stuffed sofas sat opposite one another. Their arms might be worn, but she loved their comfortable blue seating. The small lamp she'd left on cast a reassuring glow around the newly painted walls of cream and gold. Her confidence grew. She took hold of his hand as she pulled him inside. With her back to the door, she closed it behind her.

"Coffee?"

"No. Coffee is the last thing on my mind." His voice was deep, and he placed a hand on either side of her head, showing her she was going nowhere. He leaned in and kissed her. His dark lashes curled onto his cheeks as he stared intently at her.

"So what's on your mind, cowboy? I just wanted to show you some hospitality."

He gazed at her mouth and then grinned. "How about you show me your bedroom, and I'll accept all the hospitality you have to offer."

"You," she touched his smooth lips, "are one very naughty cowboy." Her hands skimmed of their own accord under his T-shirt, running up the taut, warm muscles of his chest. He felt so powerful standing before her as he watched her every move, the tousled hair on his head falling about his face in raven-black waves, a devil-may-care grin on his face. Her breathing had gone into overdrive in anticipation of what was to come. He flicked his hat onto the sofa and turned back to her.

She licked her lips. Desire pooled at her core, flowing out to moisten her panties once more. He removed his T-shirt and threw it onto the sofa.

Her gaze drifted over him, devouring every muscle. The six-pack. The V-shaped smattering of masculine hair that dipped down into his jeans. She couldn't help but notice the large bruise on his left side, and she touched it briefly, observing the wince on his face.

"That looks nasty."

"It's nothing."

It didn't look like nothing, but his hands had already slipped to her dress.

"My turn," he said as he peeled it from her shoulders.

The style of dress meant she didn't wear a bra, and his gaze lingered on her naked breasts as it pooled at her feet. She stepped out of the dress, and immediately he scooped her into his arms, drawing on the peaked tips of her nipples as she wrapped her legs firmly around him and kicked off her shoes.

He pressed her back against the door, grinding his full weight into her hips.

"Brown nipples are my favorite."

She writhed against his torso as his teeth nibbled the sensitive flesh. "Slow down, cowboy, the bedroom's through there."

"Don't you worry, baby. We're gonna have a good time."

Within two strides, he had the door open and laid her on the bed. He thrust a wrapped condom into her hand. "Hold on to that." The Victorian-style brass bed creaked as he stood and removed the rest of his clothes.

The only light came through from the living area, lighting his body with a halo effect. She could just see his erect cock, standing proud and taut against his muscled stomach, and anticipation flooded her mind at the sheer size of him.

He leaned forward and pulled off her panties. Her freshly trimmed pussy glistened from her arousal.

"Baby, I just have to taste that honey pot." Immediately, he spread her legs apart and ran his fingers over her wet folds. Using both thumbs he opened her sex to his tongue, and lashed her clitoris so slowly that she thought she would expire. Her whole body writhed from the delicious feeling.

A moan escaped her lips as he did it again. Dear heaven above, of the nine years she'd known Rob, he'd never done this to her.

She panted uncontrollably as he thrust two fingers deep into her pussy and sucked on her clitoris. A whimper escaped, as she crested on the very edge of orgasm. Then he withdrew and did it again, sucking and stroking her entire slit with his tongue. The pressure built, burning from deep inside, moving higher until she moaned in pleasure as her orgasm finally took hold. Spasm after delicious spasm racked through her body, making her arch up off the bed.

He moved up and stared down into her face as the aftershocks still flowed fiercely inside her. His weight transferred to his strong arms at either side of her.

"Now I get to look into your beautiful eyes while I fuck you."

She ran her hands up his torso, feeling the magnificent form of his muscles as he nestled between her legs.

"Hurry," she whispered as he took the condom from her grasp and ripped the packet open with his teeth.

He rolled the condom down the length of his shaft then positioned the tip right at her moist entrance. His breathing was as ragged as her own. He wiped a hand across his mouth as he looked at her. Then he grasped both her hands and held them above her head. The muscles on his whole body perfectly defined and taut, as he stared straight into her eyes.

Pinned beneath him, her breathing all erratic, she asked, "What are you waiting for, cowboy?"

Chapter Four

"Anticipation, baby. It's the best aphrodisiac around."

He was right. Her whole body craved the final act of completion. Her pussy ached with desire. "Fast or slow, Zack, just fuck me, please."

Slowly, inch by inch by inch, he sunk into her. She'd never felt so stretched. Fuck, he was big. As nerves popped and swelled, she arched against his chest, feeling the masculine hair on his torso and abdomen rasp sexily against her own skin. The rhythm he chose was agonizingly slow, withdrawing almost completely before thrusting deep inside her once more.

"Ash, baby," he whispered, "I knew you were small, but you are so fucking tight."

She threw her head back and laughed at his comment. "I knew you were big, Zack, but I didn't think I'd feel so satisfied."

He smiled.

She had to keep it casual. He hadn't led her on. There would be no tomorrow, only tonight. Why take it seriously?

He looked down into her eyes, his whole body rising above hers, mesmerizing her with slow, deliberate movements. His stomach muscles contracted and flexed as he ground his hips repeatedly into hers. She let her gaze drift down his torso to where they joined so intimately together. His cock slid unrelentingly inside her, stroke after delicious stroke. Filling her, over and over again.

The pressure had reached breaking point. Like a giant tide, the slow waves rolled in. Her pussy muscles clamped tightly around his hard cock as it pulsed inside her. With his hands still clasped around her wrists, she arched against him, enjoying the feeling of losing control.

"Zack," she whimpered as her orgasm finally shattered inside her.

"Hold on tight, baby." Releasing her hands, he raised the tempo, thrusting into her with a deep satisfaction etched on his face. As delicious aftershocks convulsed around his cock, he kissed her lips, driving his tongue into her mouth.

"You like this?" He thrust into her.

"God, yes! Harder, Zack."

"Like that?"

"Mmm, yes." Her lips parted and her head tipped back.

Ash ran her hands down his back, her long fingernails scoring the tender flesh, making it bleed. She felt each delicious thrust of his body into hers. The pressure had risen again, and she cupped his buttocks, drawing him closer still.

He stared into her eyes with each flex of his hips. His tongue swept across her mouth.

"Is that hard enough, baby?"

"Oh, more, Zack, more."

He pumped his cock deep within her, faster and faster. His balls banged against her ass, with each masculine lunge of his body. He looked so powerful as he pounded his man meat repeatedly inside her.

Arching up, another orgasm slammed into her, making her gasp and moan in complete satisfaction. Unbelievably, her climax continued until Zack reached his own shuddering peak as he spurted his goodness deep inside her.

Their breathing remained heavy until he eventually rolled off her body. After removing the condom, he kissed her cheek and lay on the bed next to her. She wondered for a minute if he'd get up and leave, but he put his arm around her shoulders and pulled her into his embrace.

"You're not how I imagined an English woman to be. Aren't you all supposed to be sexually repressed?"

"We don't all drink tea and eat scones and jam."

He laughed. "Glad to hear it, baby."

* * * *

When Zack awoke early the next morning, he looked around, uncertain where he was.

Then he remembered Ash, the English woman. He turned over in the bed, and her bare back and cute little ass filled his vision.

Yeah, he'd had a very energetic night, as he recalled. Four times he'd performed. It wasn't a record for him, but it sure as hell beat sleeping on his own. He wondered if he should wake her for round five, but he glanced at his watch and decided he had to make a move.

He slipped quietly from the bed so as not to wake her. As he searched for his clothes, he thought of how open she'd been. So giving, and loving, too. It had been a long time since he'd felt so relaxed with a woman. He knew it was because she'd taken him at face value. No questions asked. A one-night stand. No expectations, and that suited him just fine.

After dressing, he took one last look at her lying in the bed. Should he wake her? Would the questions start if he did? He decided against it.

He made a mental note of the curve of her body and her chestnut hair flowing freely over her shoulders. In another life, he would have liked to get to know her better, but becoming involved was not an option for him right now.

He turned to leave, but her voice arrested his movements. "Don't forget to close the door on your way out."

"Ash, I thought you were still sleeping."

"Thought or hoped?" She rolled over and grabbed the sheet to partially cover her naked body, the cold light of day bringing the old inhibitions back. "I know you haven't left me your phone number."

Now the recriminations had started. He sat on the bed and stroked his hand over her face, brushing the stray hairs behind her ears. Her eyes were wide and accusing, and he wondered if she would start crying. Though deep down he knew she wasn't that sort of woman. Hard knocks had visited her many times before. He guessed she was used to it.

"Ash, baby, I had a wonderful night last night. The best in a long time."

"But?"

He breathed out. "My life's complicated at the moment." His life was downright dangerous, and he couldn't risk becoming involved with anyone. Not at this point in the game.

"How complicated?"

"Too complicated."

"Do I look like her?"

"Who?"

"Your wife?"

"Why?"

"After last night, I think I've earned the right to know. She died didn't she, when Katrina struck New Orleans?"

His whole life flashed before him. He leaned forward and rested his forearms on his knees. "No, Ash, I guess you don't look like her at all. She was tall with raven-black hair and blue eyes." He looked at the woman lying on the bed next to him. He owed her a reason at least. "I didn't sleep with you because you reminded me of her."

She squeezed his hand. "Then I wish you well, cowboy."

"I'll call you." He knew it was a throwaway line, but it was better than saying nothing at all.

"Yes, you do that, Zack." Her tone said she didn't believe him.

"Ash, I gotta go." He kissed her cheek, then feeling like a selfish bastard, he began to walk from her apartment. As he got to her front door, his cell phone rang. He cursed the timing.

When he opened the door, he heard her voice shout out. "Cowboy, make sure you shut the fucking door on your way out."

Yeah, he'd really pissed her off big time. He answered the call just as he closed the door behind him.

* * * *

Ash lay back on the bed and stared at the ceiling. Her body might be spent and used, but her mind was in turmoil.

What an incredible, fantastic night. The sex had lasted for hours. The guy had a voracious appetite, and yet he'd left with barely a backward glance. She just knew he wouldn't call.

It hurt.

So what possible complications were in his life? Could he be married? Instinctively, she knew he wasn't. Clearly when he'd spoken about his dead wife, she could tell he was still in love with her. Katrina had struck some years ago. Yet the guy was still hurting even now. She felt absolutely sure that was the reason why he was drifting.

Well, he hadn't given her his phone number, even though he obviously had one. The final straw came when she heard it ringing. Up until then she'd felt sorry for him.

Well, she was sick and tired of being nice. If Cowboy Drifter ever turned up again, she'd show him the door.

She rolled over in the bed and pulled the pillow over her head. Her whole body ached from their lovemaking. It had been the best she'd ever had. Deep down, she knew that if he did show up, she'd probably give him a second chance, then a third.

Stupid came to mind. This was exactly what had happened with Rob. Why did she always like the bad guys? Rob had used and abused her for years until he finally sought the arms of a much younger actress. One with a bit part in the daytime soap series he made. Just because Rob had finally made it onto TV, he'd cast her aside like a worn out spare part. Her hands clenched tightly into the pillow. She'd given Rob the best years of her life. She'd be damned if she'd give anyone else the time of day.

No, if Cowboy Drifter showed up again, she'd put him firmly in his place.

Chapter Five

Four weeks later

Zack parked the pickup outside the diner where Ash worked. He leaned back against his seat and switched off the engine. Just what the fuck was he doing here? Surely, it would be wrong to lead Ash any further into his world. He knew it was unsafe, yet he just couldn't keep away. Since he'd last seen her, Ash had remained constantly in his thoughts day and night. He just couldn't seem to shake the sexy English woman from his mind.

Two weeks ago, he'd had the same dilemma when he'd last past through Long Beach. Only at least that time he'd heeded his own advice and kept on driving.

He drummed his fingers on the steering wheel and stared into the rear view mirror. The entrance to the diner lay perfectly framed inside it. All he had to do was step out of the pickup and walk those few yards.

He knew she would be pissed with him for not contacting her, but just to see her again would make it all worthwhile. Those sultry green eyes were just what he needed after a long grueling fortnight of dealing with low-life scum.

Through the mirror he noticed a happy couple enter the diner. Their arms wrapped around one another as they opened the door. He envied their relationship at that moment. They had stability, something he dreamed of with a woman like Ash.

They sat in one of the booths in her section, and he held his breath, knowing he'd catch a glimpse of her as she came to take their order.

He saw her approach the table, a smile pinned to her lips. She looked even smaller than he remembered. How he longed to hold her in his arms, and at least feel human again.

Fuck.

He thumped the steering wheel in frustration. What was he thinking? Did he really think she'd be satisfied with a night here, a night there? He couldn't even offer her an honest relationship. Surely she deserved better than him?

He angled the mirror away from the diner, and stared at his own reflection. "You look like trouble, my friend," he spoke out loud, and shook his head. He gunned the pickup into life, and pulled out onto the road once more. "Just what the fuck were you thinking?"

* * * *

Four weeks later

Ash closed the photographer's studio door in a hurry. If she could have slammed it shut, she would have. When she'd been sent by her agent to do the photo shoot, it had looked like life was finally going her way.

Situated on the seedier side of Los Angeles, the studio hadn't immediately triggered any alarm bells. Obviously, she wouldn't come to this part of town during the night, but daytime was just fine. The rents were cheaper, so she had expected everything to be above board.

What she hadn't expected were the requirements of the job. The photographer wanted bondage shots for a top-shelf fetish magazine. Now she was broad minded, but the fact that he wanted her completely naked with several guys sporting chains and whips turned her against it.

To top it all off, the photographer had the audacity to say she wasn't getting any younger, and this was the only type of work that a woman of her age could expect to do.

So this was yet another wasted journey in pursuit of the American dream. What with the cab fares, and other expenses, she was a good fifty bucks out of pocket. It wasn't everyday you paid good money to be insulted.

Shit.

As she walked up a side street, she heard people talking on the other side of some large trashcans. As they came into sight, her eyes widened.

Cowboy boots, tight jeans, and a black denim shirt caught her attention. His broad shoulders and confident stance and the hat worn low over his face, shielding the sun from his eyes, looked all too familiar.

Zack.

After two long months waiting for the call she knew wouldn't come, he'd finally reappeared. In the cold light of day, she saw him exchange packages with two other men. They looked sinister, to say the least. What could it be? Guns, drugs? She had no idea, but it sure didn't look legit. Quickly she turned tail, knocking some empty bottles over in her haste.

She heard one of the men mumble. "Check it out."

"Stop right there." A large hand grasped her upper arm, and she was spun round to see the face of an angry man. "What are you doin' sneakin' around, honey?" The stranger seemed to threaten her even though he didn't raise his voice. He forced her back to the group.

Zack looked at her. Surprise registered on his face, but he hid it well, then he said, "It's okay, I know her." The angry man let her go, and immediately she opened her mouth to speak, but Zack intervened.

"Ash, baby, didn't I tell you to wait in the pickup?"

Why had he lied? Who were these men? They looked dangerous, and she knew they came from the wrong side of the tracks. Maybe she should just play along.

"I was so lonely without you." She put on her best little girl voice and pouted provocatively. "I need you, sugar lips."

Zack just stared at her while the other two men burst into laughter. They slapped his back. "You better run along, sugar lips, before she melts."

She could still hear them laughing as Zack walked her firmly from the alley. "Whatever you do, don't fucking look back."

"Nice to see you again, cowboy." Then she added sarcastically, "By the way, thanks for the call."

"What are you doing down here, Ash? This is a dangerous part of town."

"That's my business, but I can tell you it was strictly legitimate."

"Meaning?"

"I saw what happened, Zack." She pointed to his bag. "Don't try and tell me you've got your lunch in that package."

"Then it's a good thing you played along because if those guys knew that, they'd have snapped your pretty little neck without a second thought."

"It's drugs, isn't it?"

His silence said it all. Cowboy Drifter was a drug dealer. Fate had been cruel. Of all the people she'd met, he had to be the one running an illegal racket. Her choice in men was simply unbelievable. Why couldn't she attract a decent, honest, wholesome guy? Trouble was they didn't turn her on. It had always been the bad boys that excited her the most.

"You can let me go now, Zack. We're far enough away."

He turned and stared at her. His piercing blue eyes drilled into her. "Ash, baby, what are you going to do?"

"As soon as I get home, I'm calling the cops." She wouldn't, but he didn't need to know that, did he? The cops hadn't come to help her when Rob had slapped her about, bruising her eye and breaking her nose. So why would she help them?

"Wrong answer, baby. I can't allow you to do that."

"You have no choice in the matter."

"There's plenty of choices, and that ain't one of them. You call the cops, you'll be dead within hours."

"I hardly think so."

"They'll know it's you, Ash, and they'll come looking for you."

"Don't be so dramatic, Zack. They don't even know where I live."

"Believe me, they've got contacts everywhere, even in the cops. As soon as they know your address, you're a dead woman."

They reached his white pickup, and he opened the door. "I'll drive you home."

She stared at him. She hardly knew him at all. They may have shared one passionate night, but that was all. She shook her head. "I don't accept rides from drug dealers."

"Just get the fuck in." He took hold of her hand and roughly pushed her inside. "I'll take you home, and we'll discuss this some more." Then he slammed the door shut.

As he walked around to the driver's side, she tried to open the door, but it was locked. He didn't trust her. "I see you don't trust me," she said as he slid into the driver's seat. "Well let me tell you something, cowboy. I don't trust you, either."

He breathed out and began to maneuver the pickup onto the road. "Fair comment."

"I suppose this is the complication in your life."

"You could say."

"You're a drug dealer. What could be more complicated than that?"

He just raised his eyebrows and continued driving. Ash held her hands to her face. "I don't believe this." She shook her head. "Of all the places I had to run into you. Now you've ruined that stupid, fanciful daydream I had."

"What daydream?"

"The one where we meet again after several months, and you've finally managed to work through your grief, and you've come back for me."

He'd stopped at an intersection and turned to look at her. "I wanted to see you again. Every time I passed through Long Beach, I thought of you. I stopped once, too, but I thought it unfair to involve you further in my life."

"No kidding." Disillusionment laced her voice. Maybe he had, but he hadn't wanted to see her that badly, otherwise he would have contacted her.

"Believe me."

"No." She stared at him. "I see your face has healed since the last time I saw you. Now you look like a perfect asshole."

She turned and glanced out the passenger window. For months she'd imagined Zack strolling into town. He'd suddenly appear. He'd swear his undying love for her. Say he couldn't live without her another minute. Of course, she'd play hard to get. Make him suffer for all her months of misery. Too bad, the dream had just crashed and burned.

Chapter Six

Of all the people to catch him dealing, it had to be her.

Zack had to figure this out carefully. He'd spent the last few years undercover. After gaining their trust, he was now finally moving up the food chain. Eventually, he would have everybody right up to the very top. Then he could pull out and finally get that ranch he'd always wanted.

He glanced at her staring out the window, all sexy and sweet in her simple white blouse and black skirt. He'd seen the look of disappointment on her face. Well, at least he had the comfort of knowing the truth. Although, what good would that do him at the moment?

He wondered how much he should tell her. In this game, he couldn't trust anyone. No, he had to play this strictly down the line. *Follow the rules, Zack.* Compromises could get him killed. Just a few misplaced words, and it would all be for nothing. He would be a dead man walking.

He knew the people he'd just met would have Ash looked into. They'd want to know exactly who she was, and what she knew. He guessed they were following him even now. They didn't trust anyone, so neither could he.

After parking in front of her condo, he walked around and opened the door for her. Green eyes stared up at him, accusing. He took hold of her arm and led her into her apartment. She seemed resigned to the fact that he'd invited himself in.

As she sat on the sofa, she said, "If you want anything to drink, you'll have to get it yourself." Then she folded her arms across her chest and waited for him to speak. Any other time, he would have laughed at her sassy remark.

He sat down opposite her. "Ash, I know what you're thinking."

"How can you? We hardly know each other. We only shared one night together." Her mouth formed into a thin line of disapproval.

"Well, sometimes one night is all you need." He knew a lot about her already. The sexy way she moaned when she came. The way she'd cared about his grief. He knew how lonely she was. That little fantasy she'd had about him coming back for her had proved that. Maybe if he told her some of the truth, maybe she'd be more forgiving.

"I'm in too deep, Ash."

"Then why don't you just get out?"

"I can't just up and leave. They'd want to know why."

"So you don't want to do this forever then?"

He shook his head. "No. I want that ranch up in Montana I told you about. I just have to find a way to get out of this life."

"How did you end up with people like that, Zack?"

"After I lost my family—"

"Family? I thought you just lost your wife?"

His fists clenched with the memory. He still hurt after all these years. Talking about it was the last thing he wanted to do, but he had to salvage this operation. It couldn't all be for nothing.

He gritted his teeth. "Girl and a boy, too."

Immediately, she came across and touched his arm. "Zack, I'm sorry."

He pulled her into his arms. He didn't want her to see his grief. "They were three and four. One minute I had everything, the next minute it had all gone. Everything I held dear was taken from me."

Overwhelmed with grief, he had jumped at the chance of some long-term undercover work in Mexico. Live or die, he couldn't have cared less. He had nothing else left to lose, but he couldn't tell her that. She might blow it. Besides, she could easily be a plant just to check him out. He couldn't trust anyone.

"It was a downward spiral. Eventually, I ended up in Mexico. I met a few people, and, well, here I am today." He let the words drift. It was almost how it had happened, anyway, no need to tell the complete truth. It would only get him into a whole heap of trouble.

"Zack, I guess I can see how you got in with the wrong crowd." She looked into his eyes. "Seriously, you need to get out, and the sooner the better."

"Now I need to know what you're going to say. If anyone comes snooping around, what are you going to tell them?"

She put her hands over her eyes and breathed in. "I don't know. I can't even think straight."

"Ash—" Just then his cell phone rang. He stood and moved to her kitchen area. While he took the call, he could see her sitting on the sofa, totally confused. If she said one word out of place, well, he wouldn't like to think of the consequences.

Now, he had to go out. Shit. He had to protect her and himself. He couldn't let her speak to anyone, not yet. Not until he'd convinced her how important it was to keep quiet. The last thing he wanted was her mouthing off, either to the scum he was involved with or the cops.

"Where's your door keys, Ash?"

"Why?"

"I haven't got time for questions, just tell me where they are."

"In my purse."

She opened her purse and gave them to him. He put them in his jacket pocket then pulled her to her feet. He led her into the bedroom.

"Ash, I don't want to do this, but I've gotta go out."

"Don't want to do what?" Her brow furrowed as she looked at him.

"This." Quickly, he removed the cuffs from his pocket. Before she knew what was happening, he'd tumbled her onto the bed. In next to no time, he had the cuffs looped through the brass headboard and clasped securely around her wrists.

"You have got to be fucking joking, Zack." Her eyes flared with anger.

"I'm sorry, Ash. I just don't want you talking to anyone. Not until I get back."

"You bastard. Just when I was beginning to feel sorry for you. Well, not anymore, Zack, you deserve everything that's coming to you."

He pulled off her shoes, being careful to dodge her feet as she tried to kick him. "Just relax. I'll only be a half hour or so."

"A half hour?" Her voice raised an octave.

"We can continue our conversation when I get back." With that, he began to walk from the bedroom until she screamed out at the top of her voice.

"Help!"

"Shouting will do you no good, Ash." He went over to the TV and turned it on, raising the volume to drown out anything her neighbors could hear.

He felt like a complete shit, but he had no choice. He could still hear her yelling as he walked away.

"Not that fucking channel. That's the last thing I want to watch. Cowboy, don't get fucking killed because there's no one. No one I tell you. I'll die here, you bastard. Don't forget to come back."

Yeah, this work had turned him into a complete and utter ruthless shit. He wondered if he'd ever get his humanity back.

Chapter Seven

This was one hell of day. Ash looked at the clock one more time. Only one minute had elapsed since she'd last glanced at it. If Zack didn't turn up soon, she'd go stir crazy.

He didn't trust her. Well, she'd give him a piece of her mind as soon as he returned.

If he returned.

She stared at the clock once more. Another minute only. He'd been gone nearly two hours. Two hours she'd been cuffed to the bed. What had possessed him?

When he'd told her he'd lost his entire family, she had genuinely felt sorry for him. Like he said, he'd had everything and then lost it all. His life must have spiraled out of control until he met up with the wrong people. Well, wrong people or not, what he'd done to her was plain unforgivable.

That interminable racket on the TV was going to tip her over into madness. Of all the luck. He had to choose the channel that showed back-to-back episodes of *St. Chad's* all through the day. *St. Chad's* was the daytime hospital soap drama that Rob acted in. Seeing her ex with his blonde bit-part actress that he'd left her for was the final straw. She closed her eyes, unable to think straight anymore.

When she heard the key turn in her front door, her eyes flew wide open, and she shouted out.

"Cowboy, I'm madder than hell. You come in here right this minute and release me!!"

He appeared at her bedroom door and leaned against the opening, just staring at her. He tossed his hat onto a chair and then combed his fingers through his hair.

"What are you waiting for, damn it?"

"Ash, baby. I think you need to calm down first."

"Don't you 'Ash baby' me," she said sarcastically. "Just get your ass over here, and unlock these." She rattled the cuffs against the brass headboard.

He pulled a gun from the waistband of his jeans and placed it on her dressing table. Suddenly she felt very frightened. Just who was this guy?

"Don't worry, I'm not about to shoot you. Besides," he held up a bag, "I've bought us dinner."

"Well, that's so sweet of you, sugar lips. Now we can play house, just like nothing's happened." Her anger mounted by the minute. Surely she would explode if he didn't release her?

"Yeah, that reminds me, I ain't never gonna live that down."

"Too bad." She breathed out heavily, trying to calm herself, but it was no use with the TV blaring in the room. "For God's sake, turn that TV off. I'm sick of looking at my ex."

He placed the bag on a side table and walked over to her television. After muting the sound, he turned and asked, "That's your ex?"

She nodded. "Yes, and the floozy he ran off with. Now I've had to lie here and watch back-to-back episodes at full volume."

Zack started to laugh.

"It's not funny, Zack. Now uncuff me, please."

"Uh-huh. Not yet. You're still acting like a disturbed rattlesnake. You need to calm down some more."

He stared at the screen. "That's the woman he ran off with?"

"Yes, that's her. The blonde with the permanent suntan and fake tits."

"Well, baby, she ain't a patch on you."

"Quit your sweet talking, it's not going to work."

"He's not much of a catch either, is he?"

"I admit he's nothing special, but he's not as big an asshole as you are at this precise moment in time. Now release me. I won't ask you again, cowboy."

He turned and looked at her, his eyes scanning over her, as she wriggled restlessly on the bed. He came and lay next to her. "Have you calmed down yet?"

Suddenly, the atmosphere between them had changed. His hand cupped her face, and he focused on her lips. Undisguised sexual hunger darkened his eyes as his gaze raked over her vulnerable form.

"No, I'm still fuming."

"Then maybe I should help fix it." He stroked his hands into her hair, brushing it away from her face. Then he leaned forward and kissed her lips sensually. Although she really wanted to kiss him back, she kept her mouth firmly shut.

He pulled away and stared into her eyes, a smile began to form on his lips. "Well, that didn't work. I'll have to try something else."

This time as he kissed her, his hand smoothed down her body to press between her legs. Even through her clothing, the pressure of his fingers on her clitoris made her gasp.

As soon as she opened her mouth his tongue slipped inside, and she kissed him back, desperate for love of any kind.

He started to undo her blouse, popping the buttons one by one.

"You're taking advantage, cowboy." Her breathing quickened. Suddenly, she wanted him to possess her. She saw the intense concentration on his face as he focused on the task in hand. His eyelashes caressed his cheeks, and his smooth lips held a hint of amusement.

"Just say the word, Ash, and I'll release you."

"You'll have to in a minute, anyway. My bra's a back fastener."

He smiled. "Is that so? You look real sexy cuffed to the bed."

"Is this one of your fantasies?"

"I guess it's one of yours, too, the way your breathing's increasing."

"Maybe I'm unfit and out of condition."

"Not from where I'm looking."

"Anyway, what are you doing with a set of cuffs?"

"Spoils of war, Ash." He peeled her blouse back, exposing her black lacy bra. She could clearly see her breasts heaving against the skin-tight material. He turned and reached down, pulling a knife from his boot. He flicked it open.

"You wouldn't dare."

"Ash, baby, I dare all the time." The cool blade of the knife skimmed across her skin, and she held her breath. In one movement he cut the lace of her bra, and her unfettered breasts bounced free. His hands grazed over her flesh, clamping the nipple between his thumb and forefinger. His mouth followed, swirling his tongue over her areola and suckling on them.

"Just say the word, Ash," he whispered as his hand smoothed down her abdomen. He undid the waistband of her skirt and peeled it from her. Then he used the knife once again, cutting the skimpy material of her black lace panties, dispatching them with barely a flick of his wrist. He tossed the knife away and pulled the ruined panties from her now trembling body.

With knowing hands, he kneaded his fingers into her pussy until she moaned out loud. "Your little honey pot is so wet, baby."

His fingers grazed over her clit then slipped inside her. She arched, feeling the cuffs on her wrists restraining her movements. This was so deliciously wicked. Bad boy Zack, finger-fucking her while she was cuffed to the bed.

He brought her to a heightened state of arousal with teasing strokes of his fingers. Right on the edge of her orgasm, he pulled away.

"Christ, I want to fuck you so bad, Ash. Just say the word, and I'll have these cuffs off and my cock in your tight pussy so fast you won't believe it."

"Turning you on, is it, cowboy?"

"You bet."

"Then you better hurry because I'm right on the edge, and I don't like to be kept waiting."

She watched him remove his clothes. Quickly and effortlessly, he discarded them on the floor. He returned to the bed with the key and a wrapped condom in his mouth.

He knelt in front of her, his whole body resplendent in the dim light. She could just see her ex still on the TV. Zack was everything he wasn't. Zack turned her on like no other man ever had.

She watched him roll the condom down his veined shaft, and her mouth watered in anticipation. She could either choose fantastic, or mind blowing.

When he leaned forward to remove the cuffs, she whispered huskily, "Leave them on, cowboy, I like it this way."

He smiled and put the key under the pillow. Mind blowing it was then.

His breathing was ragged just like her own. He scooted forward on his knees and raised her so half her body lay across his thighs, her own legs falling behind him. The masculine hair rasped against her flesh, and his warmth seeped into her.

His hands smoothed over her stomach and up to her breasts, circling and massaging with deep, sweeping movements.

"Fuck, you don't know how sexy you look."

She had a good idea. Aroused to such a state, she felt ready to climax at any moment.

Looking up into his eyes, she saw a deep intensity as he stared at her body. His hands circled, feeling her skin, gaining intimate knowledge as they caressed slowly over her.

With one hand holding her firmly around the waist, he guided his cock inside her. Concentration etched his face as he seated himself to the hilt.

Her breathing became increasingly erratic. With her arms stretched above her and anchored securely to the bed, she was open to his darkest desires. Each stroke of his shaft clinked the metal of the cuffs against the brass headboard, pulling her whole body taut.

The intense feeling doubled as he shifted, cupping her buttocks and driving into her with hard, measured thrusts. Each delicious stroke sent her further and further toward oblivion.

Her gaze drifted down her own torso to where it joined so intimately with his. His shaft glistened with her feminine juices as he repeatedly pounded his cock into her. She wanted to touch him, feel his hard muscles beneath her fingertips. The way his stomach flexed and the warmth of his skin. Moaning her frustration, she arched into him.

Every movement pulled on the cuffs, stretching her taut over his legs as he thrust deep inside her. Her pussy ached with desire, a molten heat rising, burning its way to the surface. An intense spasm gripped her until finally she arched and reached the pinnacle of ecstasy. When her orgasm smashed through her she cried out with pleasure.

"Oh, fuck, Zack, that feels so good. Don't stop, please don't stop." Her convulsions slammed around his cock with an intensity that almost made her pass out.

Pleasure swamped her senses as he continued his own relentless chase to the very edge. Roughly squeezing her ass cheeks in his hands he raised her from the bed. Her whole body pulled taut. The cuffs jarred and scraped on the brass headboard, metal on metal, as he pushed her farther and farther back up the precipice until she screamed out as ecstasy took hold once more, consuming her until he exploded inside her.

With his breathing still heavy, he reached forward and undid the cuffs.

"You, baby, are something else." He tenderly kissed her lips. "It's not often a man finds a woman like you. I guess I'm one lucky son-of-a-bitch."

He rubbed her shoulders, and then kissed her cheek. "I'll run you a bath."

Chapter Eight

"How do you feel?" he asked, standing in the doorway as Ash luxuriated in the bath. She'd been in the tub for half an hour.

"I'm fine." She smiled. "Wrists and shoulders hurt, but everything else is glowing."

"I'll use the finest silk next time."

"Oh, will there be a next time? I thought your life was too complicated?"

"It is, Ash." He breathed out. That was an understatement. Juggling the truth, that's what he had to do. She looked sad. She obviously thought he was just going to up and leave again. In other words, she thought he was a complete fucking bastard.

Well, she was involved now, whether he liked it or not. When the shit hit the fan, they'd come looking for her. She would have to be protected, moved to some safe house, or better still, persuaded to return to England.

Cuffed to the bed, she'd been incredibly sexy. He'd fucked her hard and fast. From their previous night together, he knew she liked it like that. A man in control turned a lot of women on in the bedroom. They enjoyed the freedom to explore their sexuality without making any of the decisions.

He saw her struggling to wash her back. As she tried to raise her arms, she winced. "Here, I'll do that."

He moved across and took the sponge from her hand. As he began to wash the groove of her spine and shoulders, he spoke, "Look, Ash, I guess you know I'm no angel. But, since my wife died, I haven't felt like starting a relationship with anyone."

She nodded as she let the warm water flow over her. "I can understand that. When Rob left me, I didn't want a relationship, either. The thought of starting over with someone else just seemed a mountain to climb."

If the stiffness in her shoulders was anything to go by, he realized she still hurt where her ex was concerned.

"The biggest hurdle I have, Ash, is the job I do. It's downright dangerous."

"Well, you mix with the wrong crowd."

"Your being involved with me is dangerous for your health. There are some real bad guys out there who wouldn't think twice about killing a woman." He finished washing her back and handed her the sponge. "But these people know you exist in my life now. They'll want to know all about you. What you think. What you might say."

She didn't seem to be taking him seriously because she said, "So what now then, cowboy? Will you be heading off once more, to go about your business?" He heard the sarcasm in her voice.

"No, I won't be heading off. Not if you don't want me to."

"So, it's my decision then?"

"Yes."

"Did you say you'd bought dinner?"

"Yes, it's Mexican. It's in your oven warming through."

"I'm starving."

"Good. I am, too." He kissed her shoulder. "Five minutes and I'll start dishing up."

Ten minutes later when she still hadn't appeared, he went looking for her. Dressed in a blue denim skirt and a pretty white blouse, she stared at his gun that he'd left on the dressing table.

He walked over to her. He'd seen this many times before. The fascination and revulsion appeared in sync. "Want to hold it?"

She shook her head. "Is it loaded, Zack?"

"Yes, it has to be, Ash. In my line of business I can't afford to be caught off guard. It's always with me day or night." He picked it up and angled it toward her. "Here, hold it."

She reached out her hand to touch the barrel, but her fingers froze a few inches away from it. "Have you ever killed anyone, Zack?" she whispered, her eyes wide and questioning.

"Ash, baby, are you sure you want to know the truth? Because if you do, I'll tell you."

She placed her hand quickly over his mouth. "No, don't say anything. I don't want to know. I don't want to know anything about your life outside of here." She began to walk quickly away. "Let's just eat."

Once she was seated at the small breakfast bar, he placed her food in front of her and asked. "Did you get any calls, any visitors while I was away?"

"There was a knock at the door and a telephone call." She leaned on her elbow and studied him. "You don't think they were your friends, do you?"

"There's a chance."

"Why bother with me? I'm not going to say anything."

"Aren't you?"

She shook her head. "I was angry, that's all. Everyone knows not to get involved with the cops, and especially drug dealers." She looked pointedly at him. "Like I said in the bedroom, Zack, I don't want to know about your life outside of here."

"But you do want to know me?"

She looked away and bit her lip. "It doesn't make sense, does it? You should scare the shit out of me, but you don't. I should despise you for taking advantage of me, but I don't. I should hate you for not contacting me after last time, but I don't." She shook her head. "I guess you're a bastard, but you must be my kind of bastard because anyone else I'd have shown the door."

"That's good. Maybe you'd like to come with me to Los Padres National Forest?"

"Why? What are you going there for?"

"Well, I won't be working if that's what you want to know. I thought it would be a great way to get to know each other better. See if we want to continue. A sort of vacation."

She started to eat her tortilla. "Sounds good. When are you going?"

"As soon as we've finished eating dinner."

Her mouth dropped open. "You're joking, right?"

He shook his head. "Never been more serious. So, what do you say, Ash? You and me all cozy in a log cabin. How does that sound to you?" It sounded like heaven to him. Already his cock had hardened at the prospect of spending the entire weekend alone with her.

"I'm sorry, I've got to work at the diner."

"Well, call in sick."

"I can't afford to take time off, Zack."

"Fuck the diner, it's a two-bit job, anyway. I'll pay for your time off."

"I don't want that kind of money."

"Then I'll give you some of my legitimate money. I recently sold my house. That's why I'm going up country. Maybe look at a ranch or two."

"Then you are genuine about getting out?"

"Of course I am, baby. I don't like it anymore than you do." Now that part was true. The sleaze he had to work with. He would be glad when the job was over.

"Then I'd love to come, Zack, but I don't want any of your money. I'm okay."

He smiled. He wouldn't push her on that. She obviously hated the drug side of him, and he wouldn't argue with her. "Then eat up. I think you've some sexy underwear to pack."

Chapter Nine

They arrived by mid-evening. He parked the pickup outside the accommodation he'd just paid for, and they went inside.

The log cabin was tastefully furnished with a couple of armchairs and one large sofa. In the corner, a stone chimney breast housed a small wood-burning stove. A queen-sized bed dominated the bedroom with its ornate headboard, and several pieces of wooden furniture were scattered haphazardly around. Cozy came to mind.

They dumped their possessions in the bedroom, and she watched as Zack removed his gun from the waistband of his jeans. She guessed he kept it close at hand in case of unwanted visitors. Fact was the gun turned her on, almost as much as he did. When she'd seen it in her bedroom, it conjured up all sorts of images. It symbolized him like nothing else could. It meant power and decisiveness. Then she'd asked him if he'd killed anyone. His lack of a reply had given her the answer. Asking him to keep quiet about it had been her way of denial. If he didn't say it out loud, then it wouldn't be true, would it?

The mountain air was cooler, and he went and lit a fire in the wood burner, drawing the sofa closer to enjoy the warmth of the roaring flames.

"Now this is what I miss, a genuine fire in the grate."

"Do you have anywhere you can call home, now that you've sold your house?" she asked, snuggling into his masculine warmth as the flames began to grow bolder.

"No, mainly motel rooms."

"It must be a lonely existence."

His gaze flicked to hers. "It is, Ash."

She knew most of his loneliness came from his inability to move forward after his whole family had died. He could only move on if he let go of the past.

He poured himself a bourbon and then handed her a glass of wine. He lay back on the sofa and stared at the flames. "This is heaven." When he closed his eyes, she knew he hadn't allowed himself to relax in a very long time.

She snuggled into him, and he put his arm around her shoulder. "God, it sure feels good, just to let go once in a while. Are you glad you came?"

She nodded. "Beats working at that sleazy diner."

"Yeah, it sure does. I can honestly say that was the worst breakfast I've ever eaten."

Ash giggled. "Ron's not known for his culinary skills. It's what us folks in Britain would call a greasy spoon café."

He laughed. "Greasy spoon. Kinda conjures up the right image, don't it?"

Ash sipped at her wine, wondering if she would break the relaxed atmosphere between them if she asked her question. She decided to go ahead anyway. "Do you have any pictures of your family?" She immediately felt him stiffen beside her.

"Yes, but I prefer not to look at them, Ash."

She touched his arm, and he turned toward her. At that moment, with his defenses down, she saw the burden of his loss still weighing heavily on him.

As he breathed in, he explained, "I haven't looked at them in a long time. It still hurts, you see."

"I can't imagine anything worse, Zack. Perhaps if we look at them together, it won't seem so bad."

He nodded. "Maybe. Maybe, we'll look at them tomorrow, when I feel more relaxed." She squeezed his hand, as he continued, "It's funny, I feel very protective of them. I don't like showing them to anyone, as if somehow they'll be safer that way."

"They're safe now. Nothing can ever harm them again. Don't hide them away, Zack. Let them see the light of day, celebrate their life, rather than mourn their death."

"Okay, baby." He hugged her closer and kissed her cheek. She knew he was still hurting, totally immersed in his grief. Although they'd only known each other a short while, she guessed he would always love his wife. How sad it would be if he could never find it in his heart to love again.

"So what happened between you and your ex?" Ash knew he was changing the subject, directing it away from his family was the safest option.

"I met Rob when I first came over to Hollywood. I was just twenty. We hit it off straight away. Both of us had several small bit parts on TV, and we supported each other in every way. We had virtually nothing, but we were happy, or so I thought."

"You were with him quite a few years?"

She took a sip of her wine. "Almost nine years exactly. It all started to unravel when he landed the part of Dr. Ronson in *St. Chad's*. I'm afraid the fame went to his head. He saw me as a liability rather than an asset. I was ageing and unlikely to make it. That's when he started to become physically abusive."

He pulled her closer and kissed her forehead. "I'm sorry, Ash. I didn't know he'd done that to you. God, if I ever saw him in the flesh, I'd show him that men don't hit women, ever. I mean, look at you. You're so tiny. You wouldn't stand a chance."

"He'd never been abusive before. I think the guilt of him having an affair weighed heavy on his conscience, and he took it out on me.

"I knew what was happening when he didn't come home at night. What hurts most is I gave him the best years of my life, and he gave me nothing in return. When the good times came, he didn't want to share them with me."

"Ash, baby, you haven't had the best years of your life yet. Maybe fame will come knocking, and you'll achieve everything you've ever dreamed of."

She shook her head. "Zack, my acting career is over. Believe me, I know, especially after this morning's fiasco. I may as well face facts and stop wasting my time."

"Why? What happened this morning? Was that why you were downtown in such a seedy area?"

"Yes, I went to a photo shoot at a photographer's nearby. Turned out to be a fetish magazine shoot. It's just one step away from the porn industry. They told me that's all I could expect to do at my age. Shit, and I'm not even thirty yet. No, I'm knocking it on the head, it's over."

He hugged her close. "Maybe you'll want to return to England, sooner rather than later."

"Trying to get rid of me already, Zack." She laughed.

"No, not at all. Just so you don't think I'm a complete bastard, I must give you this." He dug into his jeans pocket and handed her a matte black business card. All that was on it was a cell phone number. "You can call me on that, anytime, day or night. I know it's not much, but it's all I have."

"Then I shall keep it safe, just in case." She held it firmly in the palm of her hand. It was insignificant, and yet it felt like he'd given her the world. Maybe in his world, it was all he had.

He leaned forward and threw another log on the fire then pulled her into his embrace. He began kneading her shoulders. His long fingers soothed her aching muscles as the fire mesmerized her.

"Tell me about your ranch, Zack. I'd love to know what plans you have. Will it be cattle or horses? Or maybe you like to farm?"

"Well, I'd raise some long-horn steer and have myself a breeding program for quarter horses. That's what I miss the most, horses. Renee and I were just beginning to make a go of it, before the shit hit the fan." He looked at her. "Ash, can you ride?"

"Not really. I did have a few lessons when I was in my teens, but I never felt very confident. The horse always seemed to control me."

Zack laughed. "Yeah, you give them an inch, and they'll take a mile. Well, baby, maybe we'll go for a ride tomorrow, see what they taught you in England."

"I'd like that."

"Me, too." He smiled. "I'm glad I met up with you again. You have a very calming influence on me."

"Is that good?"

"More than you can imagine."

* * * *

Zack awoke the next morning feeling the most relaxed he'd been in a long time. With Ash lying next to him, he felt almost human again. He felt part of the here and now, rather than the past.

He pulled her into his arms, and she began to stir awake. "Hello, sleepy head," he murmured as he rolled her on top of him. Immediately, her eyes flew open. "I thought that might make you wake up." His hard cock strained against her sex.

He rubbed the hair from her eyes as she smiled and said huskily, "Morning, big boy."

He chuckled against her lips, and then kissed her as his cock slipped slowly inside her. She had the tightest, sweetest pussy and the most incredible brown nipples he'd ever seen. With his hands grasped firmly around her waist, she raised herself as he began to thrust inside her, his cock reaping the pleasure of her tight sheath.

Every time he fucked her, she stared at him. Those green eyes, drawing him closer, searching his very soul, making him drive harder and harder inside her.

He pushed her legs apart with his own and anchored them beneath his. He could see she liked to be restrained, the session with the handcuffs had really turned her on. Her pupils dilated, and she arched into him.

Her moans of pleasure fed his imagination as he suckled on her nipples and pulled the hard brown peaks into his mouth. They tasted of her sweet, feminine flavor. In truth, she comforted him like no other woman had in a very long time.

He clamped his mouth firmly on hers, driving his tongue into her moist warmth. His one hand combed into her hair to cradle the nape of her neck and bring her closer still. With his other hand he reached down to her buttocks and let his finger glide over her puckered hole. It was so sensitive as he stroked over it that he felt it tighten.

"Ever had a man make love to your ass?"

She shook her head.

"When you're highly aroused, it can be very pleasurable for both."

Slowly he smoothed his hand down to her pussy. Feeling his own cock sliding inside her almost made him lose it. Her juices flowed freely onto his finger, and he rubbed them back up to her tight little asshole. She moaned in protest against his mouth.

"It's okay, Ash. Just see if you like this." He pushed his finger into her anus and held it in place. As he drove his cock into her pussy once more, she arched backwards, and his finger slipped further inside her ass.

She bucked with the intimate contact and wrenched her mouth from his. Immediately she came, her contractions so strong around his cock that within two strokes he had climaxed himself.

"Okay, baby," he soothed, as she whimpered against his chest, the aftershocks of her orgasm still pulsing around him.

She spoke against his skin. "I never knew it could be so intense."

He smiled. Her eyes were all droopy, as if she wanted to go back to sleep. "Well, now you know how I usually start off my day."

"What, making love to a woman?"

"No. Waking up with a massive hard-on. Most times there isn't a woman around to share it with. So a few quick jerks of the wrist usually take care of it, then I have a shower. Which is exactly where I'm heading now." He slapped her bare ass playfully. "You, too, baby. You may look like the cat that's got the cream, but there's no time like the present, and if we're going on that ride together, we'd better make a move, now." As he began to slip from the bed, he whacked her sexy behind once more, the sound reverberating around the interior of the log cabin.

Chapter Ten

Ash watched, fascinated as Zack rode effortlessly around the corral. With his jeans, denim shirt, tan leather waistcoat, and black Stetson, he looked every inch the cowboy.

He rode quickly over to where she stood, bringing the jet-black stallion to a controlled halt, accompanied by a cloud of dust. "Yeah, he'll do fine," he said to the ranch hand. "Now we need something for the lady, preferably a mare with an even temperament."

"I got just the thing, mister. She's gettin' on a bit, but she won't give you any trouble." With that he walked over to an adjacent paddock, leaving Ash to stare at Zack like a love-struck schoolgirl.

He made love differently than the other men she'd known. He always managed to add an extra level of sensuality, along with complete satisfaction. Zack literally had her panting for more.

"You look at home," she said huskily.

"I feel at home, Ash. Been out of sorts, I guess. I'm thinking I may get me that ranch, sooner rather than later.

"I hope you do." He stared at her for a while, and she added nervously, "Are you sure you want me to come along? I don't want to spoil your fun. I don't think I'll be any good at riding."

"You'll be fine. Remember the dancing when we first met? You didn't make a fool of yourself, did you?"

She laughed. "No, because I had you to guide me."

The ranch hand returned with a beautiful chestnut mare. "Now you can try old Molly here. She'll enjoy a ride out with Gabriel. He's her boyfriend. They go everywhere together."

"Oh, I didn't know horses had favorites."

"Sure do, ma'am, they're just like people. Now take this hat. The sun's pretty fierce toward noon."

"Thank you." Ash placed the white cowboy hat on her head and mounted the mare. She felt rather conspicuous with the attention she was receiving, but she put on a smile of bravado.

Zack motioned with his hand. "Now take her around the corral a few times. See if you feel confident enough to go out on a ride."

Ash began to take Molly around the corral. After a short while, she felt more confident and raised her tempo to a trot. When she looked over at the two men, she saw them both laughing.

She rode over to them, and asked, "Is anything wrong?"

Zack grinned at her. "In these parts, we ain't used to seeing such fancy riding."

"Well, it's how I was taught in England."

"It might be okay for a dressage event in front of your Queen Elizabeth, but over here, we try to stay in the saddle."

She pouted and stared at them both. The ranch hand could barely contain his snickering, and Zack looked like he'd just cracked the best joke ever.

"Well I'm glad I've amused you boys, but where I come from, it's the correct way to ride."

Zack chuckled. "Ash, baby, don't get all heated up. It's up to you how you ride, but I'm telling you now, you won't be able to keep it up."

"We'll see."

"I guess we will." He turned to the ranch hand. "I think she'll be fine. Any suggestions on where to ride?"

"Just follow this track. When you get to the river, it's quite shallow there, so you can cross it, and then follow the river's edge until you pick up the track back to here. Take you a good couple of hours."

"Sounds just about right."

"Come on then, Ash. Let's see if we can make an American of you yet."

* * * *

Zack looked at Ash. She'd been quiet ever since they'd left the ranch, and that had been ten minutes ago. "Are you sulking? I was only teasing."

He smiled. She looked so small dressed in her jeans and blue blouse, sitting on the back of the old mare, and that hat she wore made her look incredibly cute. She glanced at him and smiled back. "No, I'm not sulking. I was just thinking this is the nicest thing I've done in a long while. I always seem to be working, or trying to find work. It's all I can do to pay the rent. Usually I'm too tired to do anything when I have a day off."

"Me too, Ash." He wanted to gain something of what he'd had before Katrina had blown his world apart. If he could achieve a tenth of the happiness he had then, he could at least gain some peace of mind. Being with Ash this last day or two had focused his mind. He had to get out of this undercover work. He'd given them more than enough already. It was time to get his life back.

"Shall we go faster, Ash? Do you think you'll be okay?"

"I'll give it a go, but I'm sure I'll be left behind."

He laughed. "I don't think so. Don't forget Molly has a crush on Gabriel. I don't think she'll let him get too far ahead."

With that, he picked up the pace. Glad of the wind on his face and the sound of the pounding hooves. Glad that he'd run into Ash again. She was like a catalyst, the kick-start he needed to get his life back in order.

Checking that she was still with him, he raised the pace some more. Surely he hadn't felt this alive for years.

He wanted to go faster, but fearing for Ash's safety, he slowed down. She caught up with him, all breathless and glowing.

"God, Zack, that was exhilarating."

"You bet, baby." He could just see the river coming into view. "We'll dismount up there by the large oak."

He jumped off Gabriel and tied him to a nearby bush then helped Ash off Molly. As she pressed against him, he had the overwhelming desire to kiss her. Before, when he'd kissed her, it had been a prelude to sex, but this felt different somehow. He couldn't explain it any other way. He was acting like a young man about to fall in love again.

He brushed his lips over hers. She was so small and beautiful. Why hadn't he noticed before? He guessed he had, but he'd pushed the knowledge to the back of his mind. Her mouth parted, and he pulled her into his arms, savoring the moment as he allowed the kiss to deepen.

He took great solace that she kissed him back with every bit of passion that he knew she possessed. He looked down into her pale green eyes. Damn, if he didn't have the unerring desire to tell her everything.

No, he had to hold back. It would only be a few months at the most before he could wind up the assignment.

"I didn't go too fast, did I?"

"No. I guess you could have gone faster. Zack, if you want to ride off for ten minutes at your own pace, I'll be okay. I have Molly to keep me company."

"Well, if you're sure you don't mind." He stared at her for a moment. She seemed to be able to second-guess his every thought. For the first time since Renee died, he wanted to share a part of himself with someone else.

He dug into his jeans and pulled out his cell phone. He handed it to her. "You said yesterday, they should see the light of day. I'm afraid I can't look at them with you just yet, but Renee and my kids, Jed and Tammy, are on there. I had everything I could salvage transferred to it."

Chapter Eleven

Ash stared at his cell phone. She could still hear him riding hard along the track, the dust only now just starting to settle.

Tossing her hat aside, she sat back against the tree trunk and ran her hands through her hair. In one respect, she wanted to look. She was curious as to the type of woman he'd chosen for his wife. The guy was still attached even now. Then there were his children. Their lives had been taken so young. If she had difficulty bringing herself to look, what must it be like for him?

She scrolled to the first photo. A young woman smiled at her. She looked in her early twenties with long black hair and brilliant blue eyes. She scrolled through a few more. They looked so happy.

Then the children appeared. Babies at first, and then birthdays, the candles, the smiles, and the laughter. His wife had become even more beautiful as the children had grown into toddlers. The little boy had all scraped knees, and the little girl so pretty with cascades of golden curls. Then there was one of them all together, Zack holding his daughter in his arms, his wife with her hands on the little boy's shoulders.

Finally she had scrolled through them all. Their lives so tragically cut short. The last picture, one of his little girl pouring water onto a plant. Ash felt tears well up. He had it all, and now he had nothing. How fleeting and fragile life was.

No wonder he'd gone off the rails.

When she heard the thunder of hooves in the distance, she looked up to see him rounding some bushes at a fast gallop. Eventually he drew level, bringing the horse to a measured halt in a cloud of dust and stones.

It wouldn't do to be all emotional. He needed someone strong.

He dismounted, secured the horse, and walked over to her. He lifted his hat off his head and ran his fingers through his hair.

"God, I sure enjoyed that. I have just got to get me that ranch soon. I've lived too long in the underbelly of the world."

He lay down in the grass next to her and angled his hat to shield his eyes from the sun.

She held up his cell phone. "Thank you. They're all so beautiful."

"Yes, they were." He breathed in. Although she couldn't see his eyes, his mouth moved as if he might say something else.

With the silence between them developing, she spoke, "You ought to get that one of you all together framed. It's such a lovely photo."

"Which one, Ash?"

"Can I show you?"

He hesitated, so she took the opportunity and brought the photo onto the screen, then handed the cell phone to him.

He smiled as he studied it. "Jed looks like he'd been climbing trees again. He was always getting into scrapes."

He scrolled through a few more. "I haven't seen these in ages, years in fact. It hurt too much last time. You know, I blamed myself for their deaths."

"Why?"

"Because I should have protected them."

"You can't blame yourself, Zack. Surely it was Mother Nature at her worst."

"Renee was so fond of the horses. She didn't want to leave them behind. I should have made her leave. It was my decision. I feel like I let them down."

"Zack, hindsight is all very well. You have to act on the information you've been given."

"Where we lived was surrounded by pine trees. We'd created a safe place in the house, but unfortunately one of the trees came down and crashed through to where we were sheltering. I was knocked unconscious. When I woke up, my world had abruptly ended."

She touched his hand and squeezed it, knowing it must have been awful. He pulled her down next to him.

"Thank you," he said.

"What for?"

"For helping me realize I have to move on. Renee wouldn't want me grieving for this long, either. I can almost hear her chastising me. 'Now get your butt together, and quit horse-shittin' around.'"

"Sounds like a no-nonsense lady."

"Yes, she was, but she was beautiful, intelligent, and sensitive, too. Come on, let's finish that ride." He pulled her to her feet and kissed her with a passion that left her breathless. "Keep that thought because there's plenty more where that came from."

* * * *

As they continued their ride together, Zack thought about his family. This time when he'd looked at the photos it hadn't hurt so much. He felt guilty, but he knew the time had come to move on. He had a few good years left in him, yet. Renee would have been heartbroken to see him still grieving for her and the kids. He owed it to their memory to make something of his life now.

Ash was a good woman. She had helped him to make that first step. She understood that his family would always be a special part of who he was. He could never forget them.

He felt a sense of calm wash over him as he took in the forest of pine and juniper trees spreading out into the distance. He breathed in the fresh mountain air. This had to be what life was all about. The sooner he sorted out the undercover work the better.

He noticed Ash's horse limping. "Ash, baby, you're gonna have to ride with me. Molly must have picked up a stone when we crossed the river." They both dismounted, and he secured Molly's reins to Gabriel's saddle.

Once Ash was safely mounted on Gabriel, he jumped on behind her, taking up the reins with his one hand and wrapping his free arm around her waist.

"Now this feels like heaven, Ash. A horse under me and a sexy woman in my arms."

She giggled and smoothed her hand up his arm. "Thanks for bringing me here, Zack. It's been really lovely, what with the riding and everything. I know I'm not a great horsewoman, but I've enjoyed it all the same."

He smiled. "You've done fine, Ash. You'll get better next time we come up here."

"Next time?"

"Didn't I say? We can do this whenever I'm around your area. I know you don't like what I do, but this way I can separate it off. What do you say?"

"I say, I'd like that very much."

"I pass through Long Beach once a fortnight. I can pick you up whenever I've finished what I have to do." The thought had suddenly occurred to him. What better way could there be to get to know one another? He liked her immensely already, and they certainly had a lot in common, including a mutual understanding in the bedroom.

Chapter Twelve

After another half-hour or so in the saddle, they came to a clearing. Some trees had been cut down, and several logs lay strewn about. Zack brought their horse to a controlled stop and dismounted.

"We'll just give Gabriel a rest for a while."

He held up his arms and she slid into his embrace. She stared into his eyes. It just felt so right, the two of them, all alone with their horses for company. If Ash could have known how the last few days would turn out, she would never have believed it. She had gone from utter despair to outright euphoria in just a matter of hours, and it looked like Zack felt the same way.

"Zack, you've got such a wicked grin on your face. What are you thinking?"

"Come over here, and you'll find out." She giggled as he pulled her over to one of the logs and sat down. He took off his hat and laid it on the log behind him.

She stood in front of him, and he nestled her between his legs. He stared intently at her. When he looked at her like that she felt her insides begin to melt. A tight coil of desire centered low in her belly, and excitement coursed through her veins. Zack turned her on like no other man ever could.

He kissed her possessively on the lips. "Ash, baby, you make my cock horny as hell." He nuzzled into her neck, and then whispered against her ear, "Now why don't you slip off your jeans, and put those riding skills of yours to good use, right here on my lap."

A tight moan escaped her lips at the thought of it. Breathlessly she said, "Zack, someone might see." Already she'd threaded her hands into his hair, loving the feel of it as it slipped through her fingers.

"I've deliberately taken us off the beaten track. It's totally private here." His fingers moved down to her pussy, which he massaged through her jeans. She couldn't help but arch as he pressed his whole hand firmly against her mound.

"So you had this all planned?"

"Baby, it pays to be forward thinking. I'm so hard for you, Ash. I want to fuck you right here."

"If we get caught—"

"We won't." His grin broadened, as she began removing her boots. Then she shrugged off her jeans before slipping her panties over her ankles.

He unzipped his jeans and pulled out his hard cock. The head looked swollen, and it glistened in the sunlight as he held it firmly in his hand. He smiled as she stood in front of him, and then he began unbuttoning her blouse. Zack handled her possessively. She liked the fact that he took control. After peeling her blouse back, he unclipped her front-fastening bra, and her breasts bounced free.

"Come here. All morning I've watched you riding, now I want that cute little butt of yours riding me." He lifted her onto his lap, and positioned his hard prick against the entrance to her pussy. Holding onto his shoulders, she eased down his length. Concentration etched his face as she stared into his eyes.

His cock felt delicious, as it slid deep inside her. His thick girth filled her completely, something she had never experienced with Rob. She panted breathily as she tried to accommodate his size.

"You feel so good, Ash," he murmured as he cupped her buttocks and pulled her hard against him. Straddled over his lap, her feet just touched the ground. With her hands on his shoulders, she used them as leverage, and began moving over his length.

"That's it, baby, ride me like I know you can."

Ash touched the contours of his face, tracing her fingertips down the lines of his cheek. She felt the rough masculine hair rasp against her skin as she leaned in and kissed him. Zack was all man, and she held him closer still, enjoying his warmth, as she impaled herself on him, over and over again.

"You like that, cowboy?" she whispered against his ear.

"Yeah, baby. I'll never make fun of your riding technique again."

His hands smoothed over her breasts, his rough fingers circling her nipples until he pulled them taut. She ground her hips into his, as she kissed his cheek, breathing in his scent.

"Harder, ride me harder, show me how much you want me."

"Zack." She touched her forehead to his and looked down between their bodies. Her own stomach flexed as she moved over him. Each delicious stroke of her pussy along his length sent shock waves of pleasure pulsing through every nerve ending. "Oh, Zack, look, you can see your cock sliding inside me, all covered in my juices." She loved the groan that came from him, as he glanced down, and she smiled into his eyes. If her cowboy wanted more, she'd give it to him. "I'm so wet for you, Zack." She slipped a hand down to her pussy, and gathered the wetness there. Then she offered her glistening fingers to him. "Look how you make me feel."

He sucked them into his mouth and licked the juices hungrily from her. His tongue devoured every last drop of her moist femininity as he stared into her eyes.

"I love the taste of your honey pot, now I'll show you how I feel." A moan escaped her lips as he drove his cock up to meet her downward thrust. Her back arched and he kissed the hollow below her throat, his tongue snaking out to taste her skin. She built the rhythm, faster and faster, until she rode him hard. Lifting herself, over and over until she was lost in his musky maleness.

"Fuck, baby, you were born for this."

"Zack." She stared into his eyes, seeing the man, the person underneath her. How she loved him at that very moment.

He slipped one hand between them and stroked her clit with his fingers. Her whole body arched as an intense spasm gripped her insides.

"Zack."

"Come, baby, come for me."

Her pussy clamped hard around his cock as she made two more downward movements. His dick moved ever deeper inside her.

"Zack." Her lips stayed parted as her orgasm slammed through her. She continued to ride him through the aftershocks, her pussy milking his shaft, as he gripped her buttocks and pulled her hard against him. It felt like the most intense lovemaking she'd ever known. He threaded one hand into her hair and let out a low animal growl as he spurted his creamy goodness deep inside her.

Overwhelmed, she lay breathlessly against his body as he wrapped her in his arms and held her close. She'd never felt so wanted and needed in her life.

Silently, she gave a prayer of thanks to her agent. If he hadn't sent her to that sleazy photo shoot, she would never have run into Zack again.

* * * *

Five months later

Ash glanced at her watch. Another ten minutes and she would finish her shift at the diner.

What a crazy life it had turned out to be. Every night she would arrive home, smelling of greasy hamburgers and fries. This was not the dream she had envisaged when she had first come to America.

Happiness only came once a fortnight, when Zack picked her up and took her to the cabin. Despite everything, she had come to love him. He might be on the wrong side of the law, but she could tell he had a good heart. He always treated her with the utmost affection and respect. Sometimes, when he looked at her, she could almost believe he loved her, too. Though during the five months they'd been together, he'd never once said those three special words to her.

During their stay at the cabin, she had become quite a proficient horsewoman, but it was the nights that she loved the most. Nights filled with a passion that she never knew could exist between a man and a woman.

She went over to take the last order of the day. A man dressed in jeans and a pale blue shirt sat at table nine. His face was lined and craggy from the sun. Chewing on a toothpick, he looked up as she approached.

"What can I get you, sir?" she asked absently, her mind already wondering what she would have for dinner when she arrived home.

"It's not what you can get me, little lady. It's what you can do for me."

Her gaze lifted sharply from the notepad, and she studied him more closely. "Oh?" Her eyes traced the one-inch scar on the side of his mouth.

"It's about your boyfriend."

Now that had her paying attention. Her senses sharpened. Zack had warned her about saying too much. Better to play dumb. "Which one?"

He laughed, then grabbed her wrist so suddenly that she gasped as he slammed her hand down on the table and covered it with his. "Do I have your attention now?

"Yes," she whispered, frightened.

"There's something odd about your boyfriend. He asks far too many questions. Why do you think that is?"

Ash shook her head. "Zack never speaks to me about what he does," she answered truthfully.

He stared at her for what seemed an eternity, and she realized he was sizing up what she knew. She must have passed his test, because he continued.

"Well, you tell that boyfriend of yours that my price has just gone up. Next time he buys from me he's gonna have to pay more, okay?"

Ash swallowed hard. "I really don't know what you mean."

"You don't have to. Just pass the message on. Just tell him it was nice meeting his girlfriend, and seeing just how fit and healthy you are, and how I'd like you to stay that way."

He stood and leaned into her. Fear heightened her senses. The man reeked of stale sweat and body odor. "Tell him I know where you live. Tell him I won't be so friendly when I come calling on you again." He began to walk away, and then turned. "Tell him Ramirez called."

* * * *

Another day, another seedy motel room, thought Zack as he lay back on the bed. He had to keep his future plans on hold. He must see the job out to the bitter end. Only he'd had enough. All he could think of was Ash. All he wanted was Ash.

When his cell phone rang he answered it and immediately sat up.

"Ash, what's wrong?" It was unusual for her to call, and her voice sounded worried.

"I had an unpleasant visitor come to see me at the diner, Zack. I'm scared, and I mean really scared."

"Ash, baby, what happened?" He felt anger course through his veins. Ash meant the world to him.

"A man threatened me. He said you ask too many questions. He said you need to pay more money. He said it was nice meeting your fit and healthy girlfriend. This was one bad man, Zack. I'm frightened. I really am." Her words came out in a garbled hurried rush.

His hands clenched into fists. He was over a hundred miles away from her. "Ash, baby, what did he look like?"

"Tall, your height, but older. He had a one-inch scar near his mouth. He said his name was Ramirez."

Ramirez. Fuck. The net seemed to be closing in. Ramirez was the guy who supplied the drugs. This wasn't good. He obviously wanted more money. The guy was out of control, and he'd threatened Ash.

He closed his eyes. Ramirez had become suspicious. It wouldn't be long before he put two and two together, and found out he was working for the other side.

"What's going on, Zack?"

"I can't explain everything right now." He needed to keep her safe. "Ash, are you at home?"

"No, I'm at the diner."

"Good. Look, don't go home. Go to a motel. I'm gonna sort it all out, baby. Trust me." That promise echoed in his head. He'd made the same promise to his wife and children, and he hadn't been able to keep it.

"Okay, Zack, but please be careful. I couldn't bear it if anything happened to you."

"I will, baby. Nobody's gonna harm you, Ash. You can bet on it."

He cut the cell phone connection, and immediately started to make a series of calls. The time had come to claim his life back. The time had come to keep his promise.

Chapter Thirteen

Almost forty-eight hours later, Zack's white pickup truck pulled up outside her motel room. Ash felt an immense sense of relief flood through her body, and tears of joy flowed from her eyes as she rushed from the room and into his embrace.

Strong arms folded her against his warm, hard body. "Zack, I'm so glad you've come."

"Hush, baby. I'm here. Nothing can harm you now." He stroked his hand over her face, his thumbs wiping away her tears.

She took hold of his arm and pulled him into the motel room. "I almost went frantic. I'm sure I've worn a path through this carpet. Why did it take you so long to get here?"

"I had to deal with a few things first." He pointed to the sofa. "Come and sit down. There's something I need to explain to you. I've hated having to lie these past few months."

Ash felt a cold shiver run through her spine. This sounded serious. What had he lied to her about? She swallowed. "Are you married?"

He smiled briefly and shook his head as he stared out of the motel window. Her gaze drifted over him. The tight-fitting jeans, the tan leather jacket, the dark hair cascading around his face. He was everything she'd always wanted in a man.

When he turned to look at her, she could see him trying to find the right words to broach the subject. Whatever it was, he found it difficult. He rubbed his hands over his face and then breathed in. "Ash, baby, this is more complicated than I thought."

Was he going to finish their relationship? Had he tired of her all together? "Are you going to say goodbye?" Her voice sounded thin even to her own ears, and it wouldn't be long before tears started to flow again. She could already feel the sharp pinpricks at the back of her eyes. Blinking several times, she just stared at him.

"Oh, come here." He moved across to join her and put his arms around her shoulders. "This isn't goodbye. This is hello to the rest of our lives."

"I don't understand."

"No, because I'm not explaining it right. I had it all planned." He ran his hand through his hair. "Damn. Look, there's no easy way of saying it. I'm not really Zack Delaney."

Her eyes widened. Then who was he? Who had she been sharing her body, her hopes, her fears with these past few months? Was he in more trouble than he already appeared to be? Her voice cracked, and she barely whispered, "Then who are you?"

"My name is Zack Cantrell, and I work undercover for the FBI."

Dumbfounded, she just stared at him. She opened her mouth to speak, but nothing came out.

"Baby, don't look so scared. I'm still Zack. Everything else I've told you is the truth, I'm just not working for drug dealers. I'm one of the good guys working to put the sleaze bags away."

"But you didn't say." She felt hurt that he'd led her on. Why couldn't he tell her? He didn't trust her.

"Ash, believe me, baby, every time I saw you, I wanted to tell you the truth, but I simply couldn't, it would have been too dangerous. I couldn't divulge the truth, not to anyone. It could have got them killed. It could have got you killed if the information had fallen into the wrong hands."

"Did I mean that little to you? You must know I would never have said a word."

"Ash, baby—"

"No! Don't you 'Ash baby' me, Zack. You didn't trust me. All this time you'd rather I thought you were a drug dealer. What sort of a relationship is that? It's not one built on trust, is it?"

He rubbed his hand over his face and then looked directly at her. "I have a strict code of conduct, Ash. It's the way I work. It's how I survive."

"Yeah, trust no one. Not even the woman you made love to once a fortnight." Sarcasm etched her voice, and she watched him turn away. "How can you be so clinical, Zack?" She stared at him, feeling all hurt and emotional. Deep down she loved him, but she buried the thought. She shook her head. "I don't even know who you really are."

With her mind in turmoil, she stood and walked over to the window. The only man she had ever really trusted didn't trust her. She folded her arms across her chest, and looked outside, seeing without seeing.

Zack came up behind her and put his hands on her shoulders. She immediately pushed him away.

"No, you can't get around me that easily."

She heard his sharp intake of breath, and saw the wince of pain on his face.

"Zack, what is it?"

"It's nothing, baby." In obvious discomfort, he gritted his teeth.

"That's not nothing, show me. For once let me in, Zack, please."

He must have heard the note of desperation in her voice, because he said, "I was just trying to protect you, that's all."

He unbuttoned his shirt, and peeled it back. A massive bruise darkened the center of his chest. "Normally I don't wear a bullet proof vest, but it's always advisable when we wind up an operation. Luckily this time, I did." He smoothed his hand over the purple skin. "The vest might have stopped the bullet, but it still kicked like a mule."

Her eyes widened. "Zack, you've been shot." A cold shiver ran up her spine. "But you could have been killed." The thought made her feel sick to the stomach, and fresh tears fell freely from her eyes. "I couldn't bear it if you died, Zack."

"Oh, baby, come here." He held out his arms and she melted into his embrace. He stroked his hand into her hair. "I didn't tell you because I wanted to protect you. Please forgive me."

She sniffled. "It's a lot to take in. So you're not on the wrong side of the law?" Through teary eyes, she stared up into his face. She had always hated that side to his personality. A warm glow began to spread into her stomach. Zack was one of the good guys after all.

"I hated the idea of you dealing drugs."

"I know. It's finished for good. After your call, I knew the time had come to bring everyone in. Things were getting too dangerous. That guy Ramirez, the one who came to the diner, was the main man in a drugs cartel. He was the narcotics baron overseeing a large drug racket in Los Angeles. We think he suspected me of being an undercover operative. When he visited you he was trying to find out if you knew anything important. He wanted to warn me off by intimidating you. Put the frighteners on you, so to speak. We had the final showdown today. Most of them are behind bars, including Ramirez, and I'm happy to say, they won't be going anywhere for a long time."

"Then you won't be going back?"

"No."

"Then you won't be coming to Long Beach again?"

"No."

"Then it is goodbye."

"Ash, I've got two one-way tickets to Montana. You know I'm a real cowboy at heart. I've put a deposit on a ranch. I want you to come with me. I want us to start a new life together."

She stared at him. "I don't understand. What are you saying?"

"Ash, baby, concentrate." He angled her chin so that she would look at him. "I love you. I want to marry you."

She smiled at him. He loved her, and he wasn't a drug dealer. He was everything she'd dreamed of, but she wouldn't say yes straight away, she'd make him wait a minute or two while she adjusted to her new situation. Zack was one of the good guys. How incredible was that? A smile played on her lips. "And what if I say no?"

"I'd arrest you and force you to go with me."

"You'd arrest me?"

"Uh-huh. As a federal agent I can arrest you, and deal with you as I see fit."

"Isn't that against the law? Using your powers for self-gain?"

"Sure is, baby, but being bad is just part of my nature." A wicked grin formed on his mouth, and she leaned forward and kissed him.

"I love the bad boy in you," she whispered huskily against his mouth.

"I know you do, that's why I'm arresting you on suspicion of being in love with me."

"You think very highly of yourself."

"I do. Now stand over there. I need to do a strip search."

"Hey, that's taking advantage." Her stomach coiled with desire as he marched her over to the bed.

He stood and leaned against the wall. With his arms folded and his face unreadable, he motioned with his hand toward her. "Now strip."

With trembling hands, she began to remove her clothes. Excitement coursed through her veins, and she breathed in to steady herself. Her stockings and garters were revealed as she slowly let her skirt slip to the floor.

She began unbuttoning her blouse, peeling the flimsy material from her shoulders to finally lay discarded at her feet. Her breathing grew more erratic as he stared intently at her. When she went to undo her bra, he spoke.

"Wait." He moved across to her. "Did I ask you to remove your bra?"

"No, Zack."

"I beg your pardon? Did I tell you to call me Zack? You call me Agent Cantrell, until I tell you otherwise. Now assume the position. I need to know if you're carrying any weapons." Standing behind her, he smoothed his fingers down her arms and then placed her hands forcefully on the metal bedstead. "Now don't let go until I tell you to. You understand?"

She nodded. Her heart rate had increased considerably. When he kicked her legs apart with his booted feet, she had to stifle a gasp. This was so exciting.

"Do you always wear such sexy clothing, ma'am?"

"Why? Does it turn you on?"

"Are you trying to coerce a federal agent, ma'am?"

"No."

"No, what?"

"No, Agent Cantrell."

"Good, now we understand one another." He moved away, and she heard him remove his jacket. When he came back, she felt his hot breath on her shoulder as he leaned over her.

His hands slowly feathered down her body, running across her abdomen in bold, sweeping movements. "I hope you're not expecting any special treatment just because you're wearing sexy underwear."

"No, Agent Cantrell."

He knelt behind her and frisked her legs, his fingers gliding to the very top of her thighs. "You don't appear to have any weapons, but I can't take any chances." She watched him pull his knife from his boot and flick it open. The breath caught in her throat as he severed her panties. She watched, mesmerized as they fell ruined to the floor.

"I'm going to make a serious complaint, Agent Cantrell." Her voice croaked as he cut the shoulder and back straps of her bra, and it, too, fell ruined to the floor.

"You do that, ma'am. Now hold your hands together in front of you. You're under arrest." When she complied, a set of cuffs were secured tightly around her wrists.

"Just in case you were thinking of resisting arrest. Now bend over the end of the bed. I want your ass in the air, so I can perform a full strip search."

Chapter Fourteen

Ash did as he ordered. She could barely breathe, she was so turned on. Zack played the bad boy role to perfection. Bracing her hands on the mattress, she lay over the metal bedstead, her butt tipped in the air.

He stood right behind her, and spread her legs wider with his own.

"You'd be surprised where someone can hide a weapon. Especially a woman such as yourself." She felt his hands smooth a path from her belly to her pussy, circling slowly down to finally dip between her labia. A moan escaped her lips as he pressed firmly against her clit.

"Now what have we here? Mmm, I need to study this for a while, make sure I know exactly what I'm dealing with."

He circled her clit repeatedly with his fingers, drawing it against his thumb, over and over again, until she cried out. The sounds of her pleasure muffled into the duvet, as he continued his onslaught on her senses.

"Like I said, weapons can be secreted anywhere. So brace yourself, ma'am. I'm just going to do an internal exam." Moving to one side he rubbed a hand into the crease of her butt, and then slipped two fingers inside her wet pussy. She squirmed with the intimate contact and gasped into the duvet, fighting for breath. Zack knew exactly how to turn her on. When he pulled his hand from her and pressed it against her puckered hole, she resisted, clenching her butt cheeks together.

"I hope I don't have to force you, but I will if I have to." Against all her instincts she relaxed her ass, allowing him full access. He inserted one finger and then two, stretching her back channel apart. "Oh, God," she whimpered when his other hand came to stroke over her clit.

"You're not resisting arrest, are you?" His breath fanned against her ear as he continued to stroke her, bringing her to the very edge of orgasm. With soft, soothing caresses he circled her clit, then pushed his fingers inside her pussy. Time after time, he repeated the action. All the while the two fingers of his other hand filled her ass, and her anal muscles clenched down on them, tighter and tighter, as her orgasm grew close.

Her legs trembled, and it was all she could do to keep them under her as her climax shattered through. Her moans of satisfaction were muffled against the duvet.

Playing along, she asked, "Is there anything I can do, Agent Cantrell? I'll do whatever you tell me, you're in charge." She looked up into his eyes. Although Zack kept his face deadpan, she could just see the flicker of amusement.

"Yeah, there might be something. On your knees." He unbuttoned his jeans, pulling them low over his hips to expose his throbbing, erect cock. He held the shaft in his hands and guided it to her mouth. She licked the pre-cum off the tip, swirling her tongue over the sensitive flesh. Tasting the male essence of him.

Zack Delaney, or Zack Cantrell, he still had a wicked streak in him. He would always be a bad boy to her, and that's why she loved him. He made her respond to him like no other man ever could. She took his cock inside her mouth, sucking him right back until she heard his breathing become more labored. His hand curled round her head, holding her against him, as he began to thrust into her.

Then he pulled away. "On the bed, now. I need to fuck you real bad."

She lay on the bed and watched as he pulled off his clothes, discarding them haphazardly on the floor. Her gaze drifted over his muscular body. Every taut, familiar sinew flexed as he walked back to her. Ash couldn't help notice the still darkening bruise on his chest, and she counted her blessings that she still had him. With his eyes burning into hers, he knelt over her on the bed.

"Ash, baby, are you gonna put me out of my misery, and say yes?" He smoothed his hand down the side of her face, his eyelashes curling onto his cheek as he stared intently at her. "Or do I have to persuade you some more?" He kissed her lips before she could answer, driving his tongue deep into her mouth.

With her hands still cuffed, he pushed them above her head, and attached them without warning to the headboard, and then nestled between her legs.

"I see you like to have your own way."

He smiled into her eyes. "Mmm, I'm going to keep you here until you say yes."

"Oh, I think I can be persuaded, but only if you try a little harder."

"Good," he rasped, tracing a line down her neck with his lips to the hollow below her throat. With agonizing slowness, he slipped his cock inside her. Arching back, she savored the tightness of her body around him. He suckled on her nipples, then withdrew and thrust once more inside her. The movement pulled against the restraints around her wrists, intensifying the feelings coursing through her. Zack had always brought intense pleasure to their lovemaking, by daring to do things differently.

"I missed you, Ash, baby," he whispered against her breast as his tongue lashed gently over the areola. The masculine hairs on his body rasped against her skin. All she'd ever wanted was him. As she stared at him, she knew she loved him with every breath that she took.

She arched into him, feeling his warmth, as he drew the sensitive peaks into his mouth. He braced a hand around her waist and angled his hips as he plunged ever deeper inside her. She pulled against the handcuffs attached above her head, wanting to be as close to him as possible. She couldn't believe the feelings running through as he brought her once more to the very edge of orgasm.

"Marry me, Ash. I don't want to live without you any longer," he whispered against her ear.

Zack loved her and she loved him. Even more than that he wanted to marry her. An impossible dream had suddenly turned into reality.

A spasm so pure and raw rose from deep inside her, in wave after delicious wave. Her whole body tightened around his cock, as though she would never let him go. She screamed as she climaxed once more, shouting out his name, "Oh, Zack, I love you. Of course it's yes."

He stared into her eyes. "You've made me the happiest man alive." Stroking his hand into her hair, he looked at her with such devotion, that she captured the moment in her heart, and locked it away for eternity.

He pulled his still-hard cock from her wet pussy, and then unlocked the cuffs from the bed. "Turn over, baby. I'm gonna claim all of you as mine."

Ash rolled onto her stomach. Her breathing had gone into overdrive at the knowledge of what he intended to do.

He rubbed her buttocks with deep satisfying strokes. His hands smoothed over her back. His tongue circled and licked the entire length of her spine until she moaned in pleasure. His warm breath fanned against her neck as he kissed her earlobe.

He nuzzled into her neck and raised her bottom higher so she knelt on all fours. "Just relax, baby. I'll help you."

No one had ever made love to her ass before, and she wondered if she would like it. With her senses heightened, she heard him reach over to her nightstand and unscrew a jar. Something cold and soothing touched her anus, and she shifted slightly away.

Zack held her more firmly by the waist. "Just some lube, baby." He pushed it against her puckered hole, packing it inside her with his fingers.

"I'm just going to help stretch your muscles. That way I won't hurt you."

She gasped as he pushed two fingers deep into her ass, working them against the tight entrance of her sphincter. She knew if he tried to enter her now it would be painful.

"Zack, it feels so tight."

"I know, baby, but just breathe a little deeper. It'll help you relax more."

She did as he asked, taking in a huge gulp of air as he spread even more lube deep inside her ass. It seemed to take a tremendous effort to relax her anal muscles.

"I'm going to use three fingers now, baby, okay?"

"I trust you, Zack."

Stretched more than she believed was possible, she let out a long slow breath.

"How does that feel?"

"It feels weird, Zack, but not unpleasant."

"Deep breath, baby."

Ash drew in a lung full of air, as he pushed his cock deep inside her ass. He stayed motionless for a few seconds, giving her time to get used to his length and girth. She could feel her tight anal muscles gripping the width of his huge cock. She had never felt so full. "Oh, Zack, that feels so good."

"Not hurting you, am I, baby?"

"The sensation is so beautiful, please don't stop. I love you so much."

"I love you, too, Ash."

He pulled his length almost all the way out, only to thrust back inside. One hand caressed her breast, tugging exquisitely on her nipple. The fingers of his other hand circled her swollen clit.

"You'll always belong to me now, Ash."

"God, yes, Zack." It sounded like heaven to her. There was no one in the whole wide world she'd rather be with than him.

The intensity of the moment overwhelmed her, feelings she'd never experienced before assaulted her senses. She gave herself then, relaxing into his thrusts, allowing him deeper and deeper penetration, until she arched like a bowstring, opening herself to him, because she loved him.

"Fuck, Ash, you feel amazing."

"So do you," she managed to say, as wave upon wave of pleasure gripped his cock.

She climaxed once more, shouting out his name, until he growled and spurted his cum deep inside her. Then he lay across her back until their breathing finally returned to normal.

He kissed her shoulders and neck, nuzzling the skin with such tenderness. She knew they had shared something deep and meaningful. After several minutes, he reached forward, and removed her cuffs. "Come on, baby. Let's take a shower together."

* * * *

After their intense love making, Zack felt even closer to Ash. He soaped her body with shower gel, and massaged her shoulders and wrists.

"Does that feel better, baby? I hope the cuffs weren't too tight."

As the water cascaded over them both, she touched her hands to the bruise on his chest, and he knew she wanted to know more, but was afraid to ask.

"It's, okay, now, Ash. That part of my life is all behind me now."

"Is it?" He could see the worry in her eyes, and he pulled her into his embrace.

"There's just some debriefing, and then it's over for good." He kissed the top of her head, enjoying her softness and femininity. Even now he couldn't tell her the entire truth. He still needed to protect her from the harsh reality of life.

The past forty-eight hours had been brutal, to say the least. Three men dead, and one police officer down. The casualties of the drug wars were high. Man, he'd sure had a wake up call when he'd been shot. As he was blasted into the Mexican dirt, he'd seen his whole life flash before him. There had been a time when he wouldn't have cared either way, but the thought of Ash not knowing he loved her, had made his whole heart break. As he slipped into unconsciousness, he wished he'd told her a thousand times.

Who said you don't get second chances? From now on he was determined to tell her several times a day. He knew how close he'd come to losing his life, and he would cherish every moment he had with her.

He wrapped his arms around her. "I love you, baby. I never thought I'd be able to love again, but you've shown me that it's possible. You've brought me back from the dead. Come with me to Montana. We can start a new life together."

"I love you, too, Zack, and wild horses couldn't stop me from coming with you."

His heart soared as he looked into her eyes. He felt like he'd come home.

Epilogue

Six months later

Ash glanced at Zack as they headed out on their horses. She couldn't help but smile at him. The past six months had just flown by. They'd finally set up the new fencing around the ranch, and once a week they would ride around the perimeter to check on it.

The backdrop to the ranch was simply breathtaking. The Rocky Mountains, dusky purple and rising high in the distance with their snowy white peaks, created a calming atmosphere. They both felt close to nature, and that helped bring them in touch with one another. *Big Sky Country* had certainly lived up to their expectations.

He dismounted and went over to a post, checking that it was solid in the ground. His hair blew in the wind as he removed his hat and wiped the back of his hand across his forehead. "Looks good."

"Sure does, sugar lips."

He looked up and smiled as he walked over to her. He pulled her toward him, and she slid from her horse and into his arms. "You sure look good, too, Mrs. Cantrell." He kissed her lips and asked, "Happy?"

Standing on tiptoe, she wrapped her arms around his neck and hugged him close. "I've never been happier. Especially now you've finally left the FBI. I never want to spend another day without you."

"I'll make sure you don't have to."

She smiled. She had finally found the role she had always been searching for. To be the wife of the man she loved. Who said daydreams never came true?

With every breath that she took, she loved him. His first family would always be in his heart, but he'd made room for her there, too. He loved her.

THE END

www.janbowles.com

SIREN PUBLISHING *Classic*

JAN BOWLES

Cowboy Bad Boys 2

BRANDED BY THE TEXAS RANCHER

BRANDED BY THE TEXAS RANCHER

Cowboy Bad Boys 2

JAN BOWLES
Copyright © 2011

Chapter One

With a final flourish of the paintbrush, Rebecca Wade stood back on the landing and admired her handiwork. It looked good, even if she said so herself. The pale lemon walls had added light and space to an otherwise dark and dingy walkway. A woman's touch was all that had been needed to bring the run-down house up to her exacting standards. The roof might still be leaking, but that could all be resolved with a little time and money.

As she walked along the landing proudly surveying her work, she noticed an unpainted patch of wall. She leaned over the banister, securing her hand to the rail. Just as she reached forward with the paintbrush, she heard the sound of splintering timber. Her heart somersaulted in her chest as she saw the rail detach from the wall.

Rebecca's whole life flashed before her as she lost her footing. The banister gave way and crashed to the ground floor some ten feet below. With barely any time to think, she just managed to grab hold of the newel post. She let out a long slow breath as she stared down into the hallway.

She brushed a trembling hand across her eyes, to wipe away tears of frustration. Just why had she put herself through all this? As a woman on her own, in a foreign country, she'd been trying for weeks to make something of this wreck of a house. Surely it was madness?

To become the new teacher at the local school in Avery Grove, Central Texas, she'd had to jump through hoops. Now, she'd nearly fallen and broken her neck within just three weeks of arriving. She could so easily have stayed in England in her safe, little world. So, just why hadn't she?

She went into the bathroom and splashed cold water onto her face. When she looked at her reflection in the mirror, blue eyes stared back. An accusation surfaced in her memory and slammed into the harsh light of day. *You're cold and frigid.* The last words that Jason had spoken to her when he'd broken off their engagement, one month before their wedding. She wasn't a virgin, Jason had seen to that, but she hadn't responded to him at all sexually. Maybe that was why he'd dumped her.

Rejection was the real reason she'd traveled halfway around the world. The humiliation had eaten away at her until she'd wanted to start completely afresh.

In her mind's eye, she could see the knowing looks from the doubters who had delighted in trying to crush her hopes for the future. Friends and family had all predicted her return to England within three months. She could still hear their sneering comments. *You'll never make it on your own. You'll be back before Christmas.*

Well, she had news for them, she wouldn't be returning any time soon. She would not let anything stand in her way. Not even a run-down house like this one. Maybe if she'd had more time she would have seen the house for what it was and steered clear of it. But with the new school term looming, and the deadline to begin work, she'd picked it up cheap at an auction. Now that she'd bought it, she had no choice but to make the best of it.

Perhaps the reason for all this madness was perfectly simple. In a different country she could become the woman she'd always wanted to be. At the age of twenty-eight, she felt her chances of that happening in England were practically zero. Her father had taught her to hold everything in check. To show one's true feelings would be considered immoral. That upbringing pervaded everything she did.

No, she had definitely done the right thing by coming to America. A clean break was the only way to move forward. Maybe now she'd be able to show her true potential.

The feelings that coursed through her veins whenever she slept had never really surfaced in Jason's arms, but she knew they were there all the same. They lay dormant, and hidden, just waiting for the right man to release them.

In her dreams, passion existed between a man and a woman. Now that she'd left the past behind, she just hoped she'd have the courage to find her true self.

* * * *

After arriving at Avery Groves' annual county fair, Jed Monroe parked his black SUV and then turned to his daughter. "Now don't you go gettin' in any scrapes, Annie, do you hear me?"

He shook his head. How many times had he warned her before? Yet, she still managed to fall into whole heaps of trouble.

"Okay, Pappy."

He smiled as he stared at her. Her brown eyes and blonde hair were so like her mother's, it still hurt every time he looked at her. "Here." He dipped into his jeans and pulled out a ten-dollar bill. "Now don't you go losing this."

Her eyes widened. "Thanks, Pappy." She leaned forward, kissed his cheek, and then slid from the car.

"Don't you go spendin' it on any nonsense, either," he called after her. He watched her running off, her hair flowing behind her, as she raced to meet her friends.

Truth was, since Marlene had died giving birth to her, he'd tried to bring Annie up the best he could. Just over eight years he'd managed on his own, but he knew that as she grew older, she would need the guidance of a woman. Someone she could look up to and confide in.

All this running around and climbing trees, it wasn't very ladylike. In fact, Annie had turned into a real tomboy. It was his fault, he knew, but he hadn't quite enough time to devote to her.

He stepped out of the car and locked it with a click from the remote. Maybe he'd take a look around himself. He might even enter the rodeo. He'd already put his name down on the off chance. Last year, he had promised himself that it would be the final time, but, hell, what was the point of living if you couldn't enjoy life?

* * * *

Rebecca smiled politely as she was introduced to yet more parents of her pupils. She wondered when it wouldn't seem rude to slip away and return home. Never one for mixing in crowds, she longed for the solitude of her own company. Since she'd arrived in Avery Grove, she had deliberately kept herself to herself. Now, two months on, her neighbor had asked her to accompany her to the local county fair. *"No arguing, darlin',"* Kate had insisted, *"everyone here is curious to meet the new schoolteacher. You've really fired up our imagination, what with coming from England an' all."*

"Miss Wade. Miss Wade," a small voice called, and her hand was tugged repeatedly.

She looked down to see a familiar face. "Why, little Annie Monroe. Hello."

Annie Monroe was a sweet-natured girl but needed a lot of praise to bring out her full potential. Unfortunately, Annie lagged behind in class, and although she'd tried to help her as much as possible, she feared the humiliation of always coming last would lead to frustration. Eventually, Annie would give up altogether.

"What are you doing all alone, Annie?"

"I'm not alone, Miss Wade. My Pappy's here, too. He's riding in the rodeo."

"Isn't that dangerous, Annie?"

Annie chuckled. "Why, sure, Miss Wade, but everyone rides rodeo 'round these parts."

"Oh?" As an outsider, all Rebecca could think of were the consequences. If Annie's father had an accident, what would happen to his daughter? If she were ever to fit in, she guessed she had a lot to learn.

"Come on, Miss Wade. He's going next." Annie pulled at her hand, pointing to the corral. It was futile to resist. The little girl was obviously proud of her father, and it would seem churlish to douse her enthusiasm.

By all accounts, Annie had been a disruptive influence in class. Her previous teacher had left more than enough information on the child's antics over the last year. Annie's mother had been dead for some years, so perhaps that was the reason for her unruly behavior. Though, since Rebecca had started teaching at the school, her conduct had been exemplary.

Glad for the distraction, she excused herself from her neighbor and headed over to the corral. Maybe this way she could leave early, and no one would know.

Annie slid into some wooden benches on a raised platform, just as a cowboy on a bucking bronco was thrown high into the air. He landed on his butt, to the immense amusement of the crowd around them. For a few seconds he looked winded, then he stood, dusted himself down, and walked away to a round of applause.

"Pappy's next," Annie said, nudging her with her elbow. Rebecca almost chastised her, but the little girl continued, "I'm so proud of him, Miss Wade. I know he's gonna win because I serve him a great big dinner every day."

"How old are you, Annie?"

"Eight, Miss Wade."

"Don't you think you're a little too young to serve your father a cooked dinner every day?"

"Miss Wade, I've been doing it ever since I can remember. My pappy says you're never too young to start learning."

Rebecca nodded. "Does he indeed." Her blood began to boil. Annie was far too young to take on adult responsibilities. Girls of her age should be enjoying their childhood, not acting as a surrogate wife for a lazy rancher.

"There he is, Miss Wade."

Rebecca stared over at the man slipping confidently onto the agitated horse in the enclosed pen. Dressed in a black shirt and jeans, with a typical black hat, he looked every inch the cowboy rancher. His face, craggy and lined from the sun, showed intense concentration as he took up the reins.

So that was Mr. Monroe. Already he'd intrigued her with his fine physique and strong, powerful legs.

The horse looked wild as hell, its eyes wide. It snorted and shifted repeatedly in the pen. Then the gate was opened to the cheer of the crowd. The horse bucked and reared, twisting around to unseat the weight from its back. Annie's father hung on, following the horse's moves to stabilize his position. He had natural balance and poise, adjusting to everything the horse could throw at him, his one hand held high in the air.

Eventually, when he reached the required eight-second duration, another rider helped him dismount from the horse. The crowd erupted in applause. With a huge grin on his face, he bowed to the crowd.

Annie squealed in delight. "He scored ninety-three. I knew he could do it, Miss Wade. He does it every year. Pappy always wins."

Rebecca didn't know if ninety-three was a good score, but by the cheers from the crowd, she presumed it was.

* * * *

A sense of satisfaction coursed through his veins as he walked across the corral. Jed Monroe was still king of the rodeo.

Todd and Jake thwacked his back as he started to climb over the railings to get out of the arena.

"Yeah, Jed, that's what we like to see. An old-timer showing these young whippersnappers how to do it."

He chuckled. "Fuck you, Todd, less of the old-timer." He'd known Todd and Jake since they'd all been knee-high, and there'd always been camaraderie between them, and of course a sense of competitiveness.

Already he knew he'd pulled a few muscles in the process. Tomorrow he'd be sore as hell, but he wasn't about to tell them that. He just smiled, enjoying the moment.

Sitting next to a rather elegant-looking woman, his daughter waved frantically from the raised platform. He walked over to her. When he was close enough, she launched herself into his arms, and he spun her around. It sure felt good to see her smile. "What do you think of your old Pappy now?"

"I know you're gonna win."

"We'll see, Pumpkin. There's still a few more to go yet."

"Well, I told Miss Wade you would."

He recognized the familiar name. His gaze scanned the soft features and flawless complexion of the stranger. So that was Miss Wade. Not an ounce of extra fat covered her body. Ever since the new schoolteacher had arrived, his daughter had spoken incessantly of her. Miss Wade this, and Miss Wade that. According to his daughter, Miss Wade was the best thing ever.

The woman sat ramrod straight, her hands clasped together on her lap. With her hair restricted by a tight bun, her heart-shaped face stared back from pale baby-blue eyes.

"Howdy," he said, holding out his spare hand. "I believe you're Miss Wade. My daughter has told me a lot about you."

A smile briefly showed on her full lips before fading completely. He had the distinct feeling that Miss Wade somehow disapproved of him.

"Mr. Monroe," she said, politely taking his hand in hers for the briefest of moments. Even on this hot sunny day, her hand felt cool to the touch.

Annie had spoken incessantly about her, as had the townsfolk, too. He'd heard all about the new schoolteacher coming over from England. In a small town, a newcomer was the topic of conversation for months. Everyone knew of her single status, and there had been wild speculation on that front. Some said she'd been jilted at the altar, while others said she'd escaped the evil clutches of an abusive fiancé.

Either way could be true, as his gaze scanned her from head to foot. Dressed in a plaid skirt that fell just below the knee and wearing a pale blue blouse buttoned extra high around the neckline, she looked like she'd stepped out of a Dickensian novel. He felt sure there was more to this woman than met the eye. Somehow she exuded a highly sensual persona. Yet, looking at her, he didn't really know why.

After he set his daughter down, she ran off to a waiting group of friends, leaving him alone with the schoolteacher.

"Annie speaks very highly of you, Miss Wade."

"I'm so glad, Mr. Monroe." She looked at him for a moment. "May I be direct, Mr. Monroe?"

"Go right ahead. Folks 'round these parts ain't nothing if not direct."

"I was going to telephone you for a private meeting, but as you're here, I'd like to broach the subject now. If that's all right with you?" He nodded, and she continued, "Annie, I'm afraid, is lagging a long way behind the rest of the class. She's a bright girl, it's just her attention span is very short."

He sat down on the bench next to her. A distinctive perfume assailed his senses. He recognized the smell but just couldn't quite place it. Then he knew, gardenias, she smelled of gardenias. The exotic tones were sexy and out of sync with the way she dressed. For Christ's sake, they were talking about his daughter, and all he could focus on was the perfume she wore. "Your predecessor said exactly the same thing. Then what can I do about it?"

"I propose some extra lessons, Mr. Monroe."

He shook his head. "Now I want what's best for my little girl, Miss Wade, but I ain't sure if I can rightly afford extra lessons."

Just then his name was called back to the arena. "I'm sorry, Miss Wade. I gotta go."

"Mr. Monroe, if you'd like to discuss this further, please come by the schoolhouse. I'm there most evenings until seven. I'm sure we can come to some arrangement."

* * * *

Rebecca watched him return to the arena to accept his prize of a silver belt buckle. When he had sat next to her, she had been overwhelmed by his presence.

He had a raw, masculine scent of wild horses and honest sweat. In truth, she had noticed everything about him, from the work-roughened hands to the sun-bleached hair that fell about his face. The strong jaw and smooth lips had all been branded in her mind. Yet, it was his eyes, so startlingly blue, standing out from his weather-tanned skin, which had caused the most impact. It was almost as if he could read her thoughts.

Rebecca took a deep breath. She wasn't used to this hard, masculine world where men where men. It probably came from the pioneering days when the men needed to take control and carve out a living on the land. All those centuries of hard graft had filtered down to make them incredibly masculine. The type of environment she had frequented only contained men in suits.

Jason was a suit. In fact, Jason had never even broken into a sweat. Only on a couple of occasions, when she had allowed him to make love to her, had his pulse rate raised at all, and hers had simply stayed the same. Surely that proved she was devoid of any emotion?

Yet, she knew that wasn't entirely true. Just now when Mr. Monroe had looked at her, she had felt her heart race away.

As she watched Annie's father collect his prize, she realized she had moved into a completely different world. The fact that his daughter cooked his meals at such an early age only underlined the fact. The men here saw their women in an entirely different way. Back home in England the men she'd known had seen her as weak. They'd undermined her to a point that she had little confidence in her own abilities. Here the men expected the woman to take on duties and responsibilities.

She only hoped that Jed Monroe would take his daughter's education as seriously as he seemed to take the rodeo.

Chapter Two

Jed watched his daughter playing on the swing outside the kitchen window as he put the final touches to their meal.

It had been over a week since he'd seen the schoolteacher, but every day when he looked at Annie, he remembered Miss Wade's words.

Surely he should find out what Miss Wade proposed to do? Didn't he owe it to Annie to give her the best possible start in life?

He opened the casement window and called, "Come and wash up, Annie. Dinner's just about ready." When he turned back to the kitchen, pain shot through his spine. Damn, his neck hurt like hell. He rubbed his hand over the tender flesh. Why had he entered the rodeo? He'd been suffering for over a week now.

When she entered the kitchen, he spoke to her. "Annie, Miss Wade wants me to go and see her." He smiled. "Now don't go looking so glum." He spooned a heap of corn potatoes onto her plate and motioned for her to take it to the table. "We'll drop in there this evening, and I'll see what she has to say, okay?" She started to sit down. "Hey, don't forget mine, Pumpkin. How am I meant to keep big and strong, huh?"

"Sorry, Pappy." She picked up his plate and placed it next to hers. "I like Miss Wade. She don't get cross like the other teachers."

"Well, that's good, Annie." He had to admit he quite liked Miss Wade himself.

* * * *

Rebecca placed the last book on the pile and then began tidying up. Every night she would stay after school and mark the day's work handed in by her pupils. This could all be done at home, but there was no one to rush home to, and this way suited her just fine.

Picking up the eraser, she began removing the last lesson of the day until finally it had wiped clean. Then, in her usual methodical way, she prepared for tomorrow, writing the first topic of the day on the board.

When she heard the sharp tap, she looked up, surprised to see Annie's father on the other side of the glass door.

"Come in, Mr. Monroe. I'm glad you've stopped by."

He cleared his throat. "I've left Annie outside."

Rebecca saw her on the climbing frame. "That's fine." She ushered him inside and then shut the door. Pointing to a chair, she said, "Please take a seat, Mr. Monroe."

She watched him sit tentatively on the chair opposite her desk. He rubbed a hand over his neck as he searched for the right words to begin.

"Miss Wade, I've been thinking about what you said. If you think Annie needs extra tuition, then that's what she must have." He paused. "But, I don't know how we'd go about it."

"I may have a solution, Mr. Monroe." She smiled. "I need some help around the house I've just bought. It's not in good condition, it needs work."

"Yeah, I hear you bought old Forest Tucker's place, over by Rattlesnake Creek." When she nodded, he continued, "I never seen that man do a day's work in his life, so I guess everything must need doing."

"It does indeed, Mr. Monroe. I found out the other day when it started raining. The roof leaks."

He laughed, his eyes twinkling across the divide between them. Her heart seemed to skitter in her chest. He looked at her in a different way to what she was used to. Jed Monroe seemed to look right into her soul. Averting her eyes from his, she continued, "The staircase needs some attention, too. Part of the railing collapsed the other day."

"Now that sounds dangerous, ma'am."

Raising her eyes back to his, she nodded. "I nearly fell from the landing, down onto the hall below."

He let out a long, slow breath. "Look, Miss Wade, why don't I come now and check that out for you? We can't have the schoolteacher breaking her neck, can we?"

"Would you, Mr. Monroe? If you can help, I'd match you hour for hour in tutoring Annie. I'm sure in a month or so she'll be up to speed." His brow furrowed as he stood. Feeling she may be asking too much, she added, "Would this be acceptable to you?"

"Sure would, Miss Wade. You're straight and to the point. I think you'll fit right in 'round here. The reason I look annoyed is I pulled a muscle at the rodeo last weekend." He rubbed his hand over his neck. "Thought it would have fixed itself by now."

"I may be able to help you with that, Mr. Monroe. I studied as an osteopath before taking teacher training."

"I'd be grateful for any help you can offer, Miss Wade. I can't afford any fancy doctor's fees."

Now why on earth had she offered to do that? Why hadn't she kept her mouth shut? Normally, she was indifferent to men, but around Jed Monroe she behaved out of character. Now she only had herself to blame if she found herself in an awkward situation.

Then she remembered Annie. That was it. She'd make sure Annie was there, then there couldn't possibly be any gossip amongst the townsfolk. Everything would be well and truly aboveboard. She'd make sure of it.

* * * *

"This really is dangerous." He pushed the wooden stair railing that had dislodged entirely from the wall. "You must have really had a fright."

"I did. I just managed to hang onto the newel post."

He shook his head, wincing as the pain took hold once more in his neck. "It really needs fixin' straight away, ma'am."

"So does your neck. Why don't you let me take a look at it?" Her blue eyes just stared at him coolly. He wondered if she ever showed any emotion. "If you go into the kitchen, I'll see if I can help."

Once there, he sat on one of the pine ladder-back chairs. Her cool fingers drifted over his neck. "If you could just twist your head once to the right, and then to the left," she whispered behind him. Her scent overwhelmed him. What was it with gardenias anyway? "It feels like you've trapped a nerve, Mr. Monroe."

"Is that good or bad?"

"I think I can fix it, but you'll have to remove your shirt first." As she walked over to the back door, he noticed a faint blush to her cheeks. So she wasn't quite as cool as she made out. Then she called out into the yard, "Annie, if you could just come in here for a moment, please."

He smiled and teased. "What's the matter, Miss Wade, don't you trust yourself alone with me?"

Before she could answer, Annie burst through the door just as he began to unbutton his shirt. He explained, "Miss Wade's gonna fix my bad neck, and we want you to hold on to my shirt. Can you do that, Pumpkin?"

She nodded. "Will it hurt?"

He looked at the schoolteacher, noticing the deepening blush to her cheeks. It looked kind of quaint, and to him just a little bit sexy. "I'd like to know that, too. Will it hurt?"

"Just a little."

He handed Annie his shirt and sat back down on the chair. "I'd have preferred it if you'd said no."

"I was taught never to lie, Mr. Monroe." With that, she walked behind him and placed her hands strategically, one on his back and one on his chin. "If you just let your head relax. That's it."

Then, without warning, she pulled sharply on his chin. His neck twisted, and a sharp pain drove down into his spine and out to his fingertips. He couldn't help but shout out. "Goddamn it, woman." Within seconds, the pain had diminished, and his neck moved freely for the first time in over a week.

He rubbed a hand over the muscles. "My, that feels better already. You have some real talent there, lady."

"Good, I'm glad it worked. It doesn't always."

"Me too. Fancy that, Pumpkin. Your Pappy's cured." He took the shirt from his daughter and began putting it on.

"It's a weakness in your neck, Mr. Monroe. It's likely to happen again, especially if you go rodeo riding."

"Sounds like you disapprove."

"I'm only advising. It's completely up to you what you do."

He noticed she kept her eyes averted from his, focusing somewhere on his shoulders. Damn. Close up, the schoolteacher sure was pretty. He made a mental note as he began buttoning up his shirt.

"Annie, can you get me the hammer and nails from the car?"

"Sure, Pappy." She rushed out the kitchen, leaving him alone with the schoolteacher once more. She looked small and fragile, standing behind a chair, gripping it for support. Her gaze still averted from his.

"I'll do a temporary fix on your railing. It won't look pretty, but it'll be safe. In a day or two I'll fix it properly."

When he'd finished buttoning his shirt and tucked it back into his jeans, she finally looked at him. Her eyes were huge, and he had the distinct feeling she'd been fighting some inner conflict.

"Call me Jed, please, especially since we'll be seeing more of each other." She nodded but didn't reply. So he added, "I can keep calling you Miss Wade if you prefer?"

She seemed to come to her senses and laughed nervously. "I'm sorry, I don't know what came over me. By all means, call me Rebecca."

All he could think at that moment was *what a lovely name.* "Rebecca, it suits you."

She walked over to the fridge. "Would you like a drink, Mr...Jed? You too, Annie?" she asked as his daughter came bounding into the kitchen with the hammer and nails. "I've a pitcher of homemade lemonade in here."

"Oh, yes, please, Miss Wade."

"Thank you, Rebecca. I will, but I'll just go fix your banister first." He took the hammer and nails from Annie, who looked surprised that he'd called her schoolteacher by her first name.

It didn't take long to fix, and he returned a few minutes later, enjoying the sounds of laughter coming from the kitchen.

"I'll sort out a better arrangement in a few days, but at least it's safe." He picked up the glass of lemonade and took a sip. "My, that's good."

"Pappy, Miss Wade says she'll teach me how to make it next time I come over."

"That'll be real good, Pumpkin." He looked at Rebecca. "I guess that's one thing we haven't got 'round to yet, cooking. I haven't the time to show her how to do it. I just dish it up."

"Oh, so you do the cooking then, Jed?" She smiled and turned to Annie. "And what does Annie do for her keep?"

"I serve it to the table, Miss Wade."

* * * *

When she was finally on her own, Rebecca almost sagged to the floor. Keeping her emotions in check had been an effort to say the least.

How ridiculously she'd behaved. After all, she was a grown woman, not a child. She'd seen naked chests before. Yet, she hadn't seen one as beautifully honed as Jed Monroe's. All that physical work on his ranch had carved the muscles into hard sinew. They rippled up his torso to the sparse smattering of hair on his chest.

Overwhelmed by his presence, her mind had simply gone blank. In the end, she had stopped looking at him in order to function. He must have known she was embarrassed. Thank goodness Annie had been there to divert his attention.

He really did care for his little girl. She smiled. Annie was a sweet child but clearly very literal. Well, at least now she had the truth. Finally she could put her prejudices to one side. Jed Monroe was a good man.

The arrangements they'd made were perfect. Annie would have extra tuition with her for an hour after school, and Jed would be able to come by every Sunday when Annie stayed with her grandmother.

At the top of the stairs, she let her hands drift over the banister he had fixed securely. Three large nails were hammered into the wall. She smoothed her fingers over each one in turn. In some way, she felt the power of the man soaking into her. Already she was looking forward to his next visit.

Chapter Three

The following Sunday, after he'd dropped Annie off at her grandmother's, Jed made his way over to Rebecca's.

Although he was going there to work, he looked forward to spending more time with the demure English schoolteacher. She'd certainly intrigued him with her coyness. He guessed she wasn't used to the company of men. So, perhaps it was his presence that made her act like a cat on a hot tin roof.

He could only hope.

He parked his SUV on the drive and stilled the engine, then eased himself from the driver's seat. He looked up at her roof. Yep, a whole bunch of tiles had slipped, and the chimney looked in need of fixin'.

As he calculated how many tiles he'd have to buy, the front swung door open, and she walked over to him. Her hair was still swept up on top of her head, and she wore a fetching cotton summer dress in red and white. It clung to all the right places. He wondered if she knew how attractive he found her. He smiled to himself. If she knew exactly what he was thinking now, he figured she'd quickly change into her buttoned-up school attire.

"Rebecca."

"Jed. It's good of you to come. I don't know where you want to start?" Her eyes just failed to connect with his, and he knew she was trying to distance herself from him. He put that down to shyness, or maybe she just plain fancied him.

In your dreams, Monroe.

A classy woman like Rebecca was hardly going to fall for a rough Texas rancher.

"Well, even though your roof needs attention, I can't start on it right away. Not until I've bought some spare tiles. Maybe you could tell me what else needs fixin'."

"It's best if I show you."

Jed followed her through the house as she pointed to several things that needed attention. All the time his mind remained only half-focused on the tasks, and fully focused on her. Her femininity assailed his senses. Small and petite and incredibly delicate, she was just the type of woman that had always aroused him.

The quiet ones with their hidden depths had his mind working overtime. He imagined her under him, naked and begging him for her release. Fuck, if his cock hadn't hardened into a steel rod. Now that was painful. Better to think about roof tiles and planks of wood than something that was unlikely to happen.

When she'd finished showing him around, she turned and asked him, "Jed, perhaps you'd like a coffee before you start?" The small kitchen area meant that she was standing far closer to him than she might otherwise do. She clasped her hands tightly together, a sign of nervousness most probably caused by having a man in the house. Something she clearly wasn't used to. She could barely bring herself to look him in the eye. He wondered why a woman as beautiful as Rebecca had ended up so uncertain of herself?

Realizing it might be best to give her some space, he began removing his jacket. "No, I'll start with your windows first, maybe I'll stop for a drink in an hour or so."

* * * *

When Rebecca looked through the kitchen window, she'd catch a glimpse of Jed. He'd removed his shirt, and although she'd seen his naked torso before when she'd fixed the trapped nerve in his neck, she allowed her gaze to linger on his fine physique.

It was wrong she knew, but instead of turning her head as she rolled the pastry out for her pie, she glanced surreptitiously at him. Unused to the presence of men around her, she enjoyed her covert appreciation of his body. He certainly had muscles in all the right places. How strong he must be. A tight moan escaped her lips as she imagined his body pressed against hers. So close that she could feel the warmth of his skin as he touched hers and smell the scent of his musky masculinity. She closed her eyes to stop the devilish thoughts that taunted her mind. Being alone with Jed had made her act like a complete idiot.

"This won't do," she said out loud.

"That's the first sign of madness."

The deep voice from behind her caught her off guard, and she spun around. "What is?"

Jed leaned nonchalantly against the open doorway, his gaze traveled over her from head to toe. A look of pure amusement spread across his face.

"You were talking to yourself, Rebecca."

"Oh, I'm sorry, I didn't know I'd spoken out loud."

He grinned. "I guess you were absorbed by your pie making."

She felt her cheeks suffuse with heat. Did he know she'd been watching him for the last twenty minutes?

She moved to the fridge. "I'll get you a cold beer," she said by way of a distraction. She handed him a bottle of Bud. "I got these especially for you. I don't drink myself." Their fingers touched briefly as he took the bottle from her, and her eyes immediately locked on his. Rooted to the spot, she saw amusement there. It was all she could do to stop herself from running away. What must Jed think of her? Surely she was acting like a child?

The whole point of immigrating to America had been to start afresh, yet she still couldn't shake her strict upbringing from her thoughts. It seeped into everything she did. Turning over a new leaf would be easier said, than done.

Averting her gaze from his, she motioned with her hand to the kitchen table. "Would you like to sit down?"

"Only if it won't make you nervous?"

"Of course not, why do you say that?"

"Just a feeling I get."

Her heart began thumping in her chest as he brushed past her and sprawled onto a kitchen chair. His whole torso glistened from the manual labor and the heat of the sun. She'd never known anyone so completely masculine as Jed. His presence overwhelmed her, and he seemed to know it, too. He raised the bottle of Bud to his lips as he stared at her. He swallowed the contents in one long swig and placed the empty bottle back on the table.

Maybe she should explain. "It's not you, Jed," she lied. "I'm just not used to having people around." Well, that part was true. "In England I lived a very sheltered life. America is very different to what I'm used to."

"Sounds like you regret coming over."

"Oh, no," she assured him, as her confidence grew. With Jed sitting down she didn't feel quite so overawed by him. "It's the best thing I've ever done. Everyone is so open and friendly. It just takes a bit of getting used to, that's all."

"Good, I'm glad you're not thinking of going back."

"Why?"

"Because I—" He smiled, a teasing smile. "My little Annie thinks you're the best teacher ever."

"I'm glad." She smiled back. Their eyes connected. He opened his mouth to speak and then closed it again. Whatever he'd been about to say he'd decided against it.

He rubbed a hand over his face and then looked at the array of fresh-baked goods on the table. "My, these sure smell good."

"I've baked one for you to take home, but you can have a piece now if you like."

"You sure know the way to a man's heart, Rebecca."

She just saw the hint of a smile on his face as a blush began to settle in her cheeks. Well, she'd have to get used to having him around, and his teasing, too. Annie needed the extra schooling, and she needed the help around the house.

* * * *

A week later, at the top of a ladder, Jed hammered a chisel into the rotten wood of an upstairs casement window. Old Forest Tucker had sure left the place to rot. They all really needed replacing, but Rebecca just didn't have that kind of money.

As he chiseled away, he reflected on how well things were going between them. She still hadn't entirely relaxed in his presence, but that was to be expected. When she'd told him about her upbringing, she'd given him an insight into what made her tick. He had to admire her guts for coming to the US in the first place. It must have been a big step for her.

Last week he'd almost asked her for a date, but he'd backed off at the last minute. He didn't want to scare her away. There would be plenty of time to make a move. He just needed to choose the right moment.

He shook his head as he scraped out the last of the rotting timber. If she's not attracted to you, you'll make a complete ass of yourself.

Well, it wouldn't be for the first time. No, he'd say something sooner or later. He felt sure she liked him. Her body language said she did. All those little looks she gave when she thought he wasn't watching. He grinned. Yep, he felt like a stag during the rutting season. His cock just wouldn't play dead. How fucking embarrassing was that?

He brushed his fingers over the freshly cut wood and a sharp pain pierced his flesh. On close inspection, a splinter of wood had driven down behind the nail of his index finger.

"Goddamn." Now that hurt. He shook his hand in order to alleviate the intensity.

"Are you all right? I've brought you a cold beer."

He looked below to see Rebecca standing at the bottom of the ladder.

He began climbing down. "I'm fine. Just picked up a splinter, that's all." He winced as he took the bottle from her.

"Here, let me see." She held out her hand, and he dutifully placed his own in it as he took a welcome swig of ice-cold beer. "That's nasty. Come inside, and I'll see to it."

"It's nothing."

"I insist." Her eyes flared. It was the first time he'd seen her annoyed. Her lips pouted, and he couldn't help but think how pretty she looked. "It might get infected."

"You're the boss." He followed her inside, his gaze scanning her ramrod straight back. Her hair was still pinned up, and she wore jeans and a pretty blue blouse. He couldn't help but linger on her cute little butt. Rebecca sure was a prize worth winning.

"If you sit there," she pointed to a chair, "I'll just get some antiseptic." She disappeared down the hallway and returned moments later with a bottle and a small towel.

"Hold out your hand."

"Yes, nurse."

A faint smile brushed her lips as she held his hand in hers. Then she produced a pair of tweezers.

"Give me those. I can do that."

"Ah, scared I might hurt you?"

"Nope."

"Good, then I'll do it, it'll be less painful."

He could just see the slight hesitancy before she leaned closer. He studied her face. Her dark lashes curled down onto her pale skin. He'd never noticed before, but she had the teeniest freckles scattered across the bridge of her nose.

"Those are cute."

"What are?"

"Those little freckles on your nose."

Color rose in her cheeks, and she flicked her gaze momentarily to his. "Jed, I need to concentrate. This might hurt," she said, as she clamped the tweezers around the offending splinter.

He hardly noticed as she pulled it from his finger. All he could focus on was her. Her unmistakable perfume. Her full lips. Fuck, he wanted to pull her into his arms right now and kiss those lips. She must have guessed his thoughts because she quickly moved away, putting space between them.

"You'd better put some antiseptic on it."

"Aren't you going to do it?" he asked.

"I'm sure you can do that yourself." She looked distracted and then turned quickly toward the sink and stared out the window. Her hand moved across her face and then brushed nervously into her hair.

Surely she must guess his intentions by now. "Rebecca, I want—"

"Oh, my washing, it's raining." With that, she dashed outside, leaving him on his own. When he looked out the window, he couldn't see a damn drop of rain. All he saw was a clear blue sky and not a cloud in sight.

She certainly wasn't making this dating game easy for him. Now he'd have to find another time to ask her. Still, there was no doubt in his mind that she wanted him as much as he wanted her.

Chapter Four

Two weeks later

Rebecca removed the apple pie from the oven and placed it on the cooling wire. In a couple of minutes, she'd call Jed in for a drink. He'd been on the roof for the past couple of hours. Every now and then, she heard a hammer hitting home. The sun was quite fierce, and she knew he would be thirsty.

She poured a drink and went outside. Unable to see him, she called out, "Jed, there's a beer waiting for you."

"Okay, be right down." His disembodied voice returned from the roof.

Sitting at the table, Rebecca sipped at her cool lemonade. When Jed walked in, her heart seemed to stop working. Naked from the waist up, sweat glistened on his tanned torso as he washed his hands in the sink. "Something sure smells good."

With her concentration focused on Jed, the glass slipped from her fingers and shattered noisily on the tiled floor, breaking into a thousand pieces. "Oh. How clumsy of me."

Just as she bent down to tidy up, he did, too. "Watch you don't cut yourself, Rebecca."

His hand accidentally brushed against hers as he reached for a large piece of glass. She looked up into startlingly blue eyes. His gaze slipped to her mouth, and she couldn't help but lick her lips. His perfectly toned body rippled with muscles mere inches from her. All she had to do was reach out and touch him.

He spoke. "Rebecca, I—"

"I'll get a brush," she hastily interrupted. Getting quickly to her feet, she went and retrieved a dustpan and brush from the broom cupboard. Better to deny the attraction between them than to start something that would only lead to disappointment.

It had been like this for the last couple of visits. Every time they were alone together, this feeling would consume her like nothing she had known before.

"Rebecca, I've been coming here for the last month. There's an attraction between us. I feel it, and I know you feel it, too."

With an effort she barely thought possible, she looked him straight in the eye. Confusion reflected on his features as he held her gaze. Denial would be the safest option. "I don't know what you mean, Jed. Surely you know I'm not your type."

He laughed, his brows drawing together as he studied her. "And what type are you?"

"I don't know. I've been told I'm too cold. What type would you suggest? Ice queen? Ice maiden?" She began sweeping the shards of glass into the dustpan with exaggerated movements. Anything to keep herself from looking at him.

"Who told you that?"

"My ex-fiancé."

"I see."

"No, I don't think you do. My father was a vicar. A preacher, if you like. I've got plenty of hang-ups that would make you unhappy."

"Is that why you came to America? To escape your father?"

Lifting her head from her task, she stared at him. His piercing gaze held her captive. It was all she could do to keep breathing. Surely he was the most attractive man she'd ever seen? "My father's been dead for two years now. I came to America to leave the humiliation of rejection behind. I don't wish to add any more."

"So you'd rather reject me, Rebecca, than have some fun?"

"I'm sorry. It's for the best." All her emotions surfaced as she put the brush and pan to one side. She would always be a failure where men were concerned. She'd hoped to leave the past behind her, but she just didn't seem to have the courage to make that final step. The idea that she would be a disappointment to any man scared her the most. She just couldn't deal with the humiliation again.

"What are you frightened of, Rebecca?"

"I'm not frightened." She moved out of his reach. "How about some apple pie?"

"Instead of you, you mean? I don't think you're taking anything I say seriously."

Without warning he pressed her hard against the kitchen table. Taking her hands in his, he pinned them down on either side of her. His gaze focused on her mouth, her own eyes unable to ignore the pure masculine presence of him. The hard contours of his chest, so close and overwhelming, made the breath seize in her lungs in a short, sharp gasp.

He leaned forward, his warm breath fanning against her neck as he whispered softly in her ear. "I see I've got your attention, Rebecca, because you've sure as hell had mine these past few weeks."

"Jed." He felt so incredibly sexy standing right up against her. His heat soaked through the dress she wore. His male scent pervaded her senses like nothing she had known before. "Believe me, I'm the complete opposite to you."

"I don't think so. I've seen you looking at me when you think I don't notice. There's a connection between us. You want me, just as much as I want you."

"You are mistaken."

"Uh-uh." He brushed his lips against her cheek, his mouth nuzzling her soft skin as he tasted a line to her ear. Pressed back against the table, her hands pinned beneath his, she could barely move. It excited her like never before. "Truth be known, you'd like me to take you here, on this table, right now, and fuck you senseless."

The image and the language he used shocked and startled her. No one had ever spoken to her like that before. Jason had never been as crude as that. Trouble was, Jed turned her on far more than Jason ever could. Maybe Jed was right. Maybe she was more like him than she realized.

Only a few base words wouldn't begin to change a whole lifetime of concealment. To allow Jed in, she would have to let her defenses down, and she just wasn't ready to do that. She liked her safe little world. That way she wouldn't disappoint herself or anyone else.

"As I said, Jed. You are mistaken. Now let me go."

He stared at her for a moment. "Very well." Then he leaned in and whispered low against her ear. "You may fool everyone else. You may even fool yourself, but you can't fool me. Maybe you need a man like me, rather than that dickless wonder back in England. I bet your father approved of him."

She looked sharply at him. He'd hit the nail on the head. "He did."

"Well, darlin', he would never have approved of me." With that, he moved away and went back outside, leaving her feeling incredibly empty. Jed had given her plenty to think about.

* * * *

Jed pulled into the parking lot outside Madison's and stilled the engine. Usually he looked forward to a couple of beers on a Sunday night with Todd and Jake, but not tonight.

His thoughts were consumed with Rebecca. He'd begun to form an attachment to her. He guessed it was the time they'd spent together. He knew her quite well. He shook his head. He knew diddly-squat because she just wouldn't let him in.

This afternoon she had looked so scared when he'd suggested there was a mutual attraction between them. Like a deer caught in the headlights, she had just stared back at him. Frightened of stepping across the divide between them.

He didn't think for one minute that she was that cold, passionless woman she had described herself as. No wonder she had left England.

The men in her life had completely destroyed her self-confidence. He knew Rebecca had a lot to give. He just had to find a way to coax it from her.

He entered the bar and walked over to his drinking buddies. They grinned at him as he approached.

"You finally made it then, Jed. Jake and I had our doubts that you'd turn up this evening."

"And why is that, Todd?"

"We heard through the grapevine that you've been slipping the new schoolteacher a length."

"Fuck you, Todd." This was all he needed. The townsfolk of Avery Grove were there when you needed them, like when he'd first lost his wife. But by God, they took an unholy interest in everyone's love life, or lack of it.

He ordered three beers, noticing their reflections in the mirror behind the bar. "If you two don't stop smirking, I'm outta here."

"Well, you can confide in us, Jed. We won't tell a soul."

"Sure. How about I tell you zilch?" He took a swig of his beer, feeling rather defensive about Rebecca.

"That's too bad, Jed," Jake teased. "We all heard you'd nailed her in the kitchen."

He shook his head in amusement. "Such details, where do you get your information from?"

Todd joined in. "Apparently, as soon as you got inside her house, you ripped each other's clothes off, and then you got inside her."

Jed started to laugh. "I hate to disappoint you, but I think my little Annie has something to do with the rumors. I'm afraid she's misconstrued what's happening. You know what kids are like, two and two make six." He really ought to have a word with her, but if he did, wouldn't he be fueling the gossip?

"Well that ain't no good to you, Jed. The whole town thinks you're fucking her. It's the major topic of conversation all over."

"Great." He began to walk from the bar. He at least ought to warn Rebecca before she heard the rumors herself.

"Hey, where are you going?" Jake called after him.

He gave the finger, and Todd added, "I sure hope she's keeping it nice and warm for you."

* * * *

Rebecca ran the brush through her waist-length hair one more time. Sunday nights were her pamper nights. A long bath followed by liberal amounts of lotions and potions.

Some soft background music played on the radio, and as soon as the program finished, she'd retire to bed. It was an early start again tomorrow.

When the doorbell rang, she pulled the dressing gown around herself and did up the tie.

"Who is it?" she called, not wanting to open the door this late.

"Rebecca, it's Jed."

Her heart began to beat faster. Her hand shook as her fingers grasped the lock. What did he want at this late hour? "Can't it wait until morning, Jed?"

She heard his slow exhale of breath. "Rebecca, we need to talk. Trust me, I'm not gonna try anything."

Trust him? Did she trust him? Maybe she did, but she certainly didn't trust herself where he was concerned.

As she swung the door open, she leaned against the wall, needing some support to steady herself. Dressed in jeans and a red check shirt with a tan leather jacket, he looked every inch the cowboy. Holding his hat in his hands, his sun-bleached hair was all ruffled as if he'd just run his hands through it.

His gaze drifted over her, taking in her bare feet and scantily clad body. It wouldn't take a genius to work out what he was thinking.

Swallowing hard, she ushered him inside. "Would you like a drink, Jed?"

He shook his head. "No, I better not stay. I thought you ought to know that there're some rumors flying around about us."

"Oh? What sort of rumors?" He towered over her and seemed to fill her entire living room with his brooding, masculine presence. She could just see the first signs of stubble on his jaw. Fighting the urge to run her hands over his skin, she sought safety and pressed her back against the wall again.

"The whole town thinks we're an item. I found out this evening when I went out. I just thought I should warn you, that's all."

"That explains the strange looks I received in the grocery store on Friday. I thought Mrs. Gayle looked at me rather too closely."

He chuckled. "That old busybody is the hub of gossip in these parts. If you want something broadcast, just go to her. You don't seem as upset as I thought you might."

Rebecca drew her brows together. She wasn't in the least worried. She smiled. "No, I'm sure they've been gossiping about me ever since I arrived. It's not the end of the world. Besides, we know it isn't true."

He let out a long, slow breath and turned away from her, running his hand roughly through his hair.

"What is it, Jed?" she asked, already knowing the reason for his behavior. Her heart ached it was beating so fast.

"I wish it were true, Rebecca." He took one step toward her, his gaze dark and piercing as he looked at her. Reaching out a hand, he touched the hair that fell loosely about her shoulders. "You look real pretty with your hair down. You should always wear it like this." He wound the strands into his fingers, twisting them until his hand caressed the side of her cheek.

Transfixed, she just stared at him, unable to move, unable to speak. Just the pounding of her own racing heart in her ears. Her unsteady breaths forced her lips to part, and she gasped for air.

"Rebecca, you're such a hard nut to crack," he whispered, the deep timbre of his voice mesmerizing.

Without really knowing why, she briefly closed her eyes and snuggled against his tender touch. Somehow he felt safe and strong, and he made her feel less lonely.

He moved his hand to the nape of her neck, his fingers meshing into her hair. She wanted him to kiss her. She wanted to know how it felt when you kissed a man that made your knees go weak whenever you were in his presence. He was so close now. As she leaned back against the wall, she noticed his eyelashes caressing down onto his cheeks as he stared intently at her.

He spun his hat onto a nearby chair and pressed his lips to hers. Her sharp intake of breath confirmed her suspicions. No one had ever kissed her like this before. Of their own accord, her hands teased into his hair, running through the golden strands, enjoying the feeling of his soft locks against her fingertips.

His other hand circled her waist, and he pressed his hard, taut body against hers, pinning her where she stood. Overwhelmed by him, she did something she had never done before, and she kissed him back with a passion she had only ever read about.

A moan tore from her, and she nipped at his mouth with her teeth, running her tongue over his lips as they molded their bodies together. A million nerve endings exploded, heightening her senses. His masculine scent filled her lungs, and she breathed in deeply, wanting more. His heat enveloped her, burning into her, and she pressed against him, needing more. God, how she needed more. It hurt to want and not receive.

You're nothing but a heathen and a harlot. Her father's words forced their way into her brain. They didn't belong there, and she pushed them away, but they returned, this time more forcefully. *Jezebel, strumpet. Hell and damnation awaits those who sin.* She didn't believe it. How long had it been since she had even gone to church? Her father's doctrine over the years had eventually turned her from religion. Better to seek one's own peace with God by being a decent member of society. No need for sermons, but it brought her back to reality with a sharp bang. This was so unlike her.

Chapter Five

Just when he thought he'd finally got through to her, she pushed him away. Her eyes were wild as she stared at him, her breathing as heavy as his own.

"I'm sorry, Jed. I don't know what came over me. That's not at all like me."

He placed both his hands against the wall, on either side of her head. He wouldn't give up without a fight. "Maybe that's the real you, only you've never allowed yourself to express it before."

She shook her head, a knot of confusion on her brow. "No, I assure you, I've never acted like that with anyone."

While a sense of satisfaction washed over him that she had given him a part of herself, he wondered if the reason for her change of heart was far simpler. He stroked a hand into her silky soft hair, pushing the strands back from her face. "Rebecca, if you're a virgin, just say."

A strangled laugh escaped her lips as her eyes flew to his. "I'm twenty-eight, no." She bit her lip. "But I'm acting like one. I must be, or you wouldn't have said it."

"You're just scared to be yourself, that's all."

"I'm pathetic." Irritated with herself, she pushed past him and walked to the door. With her eyes downcast, she whispered, "Maybe you should go, Jed. I can't give you what you want."

"I disagree." When Rebecca had opened the door to him, she'd taken his breath away. Dressed in a silk robe and with her hair flowing around her shoulders, he had seen her pure beauty for the first time. Immediately he had wanted to pull her into his arms and kiss her with an urgent desire that had consumed him these past few weeks.

Now that they'd kissed, there was no way he would just walk away. He wanted her now more than ever. If that meant coaxing and cajoling for the next millennium, then that's what he would do.

"I like you, Rebecca. You're a very passionate woman. All you have to do is let go of the past."

"I thought I'd left it all behind in England, but it seems I brought that emotional baggage with me." She looked at him. "I'm sorry I've disappointed you."

He kissed her cheek. "You haven't disappointed me one bit. Now I know your hidden depths. There's no way I'm giving up."

"Really?"

Her fragility overwhelmed him. "Yes, really. I'm not as selfish as you think."

She walked with him to the door. He turned to her and smiled. "I'll see you in the week when I pick Annie up from school."

"Jed." Her hand touched his. "I do like you, Jed."

"That's good. You know I like you, too."

He saw the inner turmoil on her features as she fought for the right words to say. "I've never felt like this with a man before."

He nodded. That was a good sign. "Do you want me to stay?"

"I want you to stay, but if I said I was scared, would you think me an idiot? Because I feel like one."

"No, of course not." All he saw was a beautiful, vulnerable woman who just needed to find herself. "Rebecca, there's nothing more I wanna do than spend time with you, but if I walk back through this door, I want you to know I won't be leaving 'til daybreak."

* * * *

With his eyes burning into hers, he walked back inside. He tossed his hat aside and immediately pulled her into his arms. His kiss, rough and possessive, branded her lips.

As she melted into him, he caressed her face, her neck. He stroked a hand into her hair as he whispered against her ear, "I wanna fuck you real bad, Rebecca."

"Jed, do you have to be so crude?"

"I'm just a Texas rancher, darlin'. I don't have any fancy words to woo you with. But I'm thinking you like the way I talk. You just won't admit it yet."

Powerful and strong, he turned her on like no other man ever had. When he lifted her into his arms, her pulse rate increased. He played her caveman fantasy with relish.

"I guess you know where my bedroom is," she whispered against his neck, "since you've repaired every window in the house."

He grinned. "And very nice it is, too. The perfect place to get to know each other better."

She giggled as he took the stairs two at a time. Her weight seemed to mean nothing to him. The man had an energy she found exhilarating.

When the door finally closed behind them, she flicked on a switch, bathing the room in subdued light from the lamps either side of her bed. Everything familiar to her soothed her nerves. The brass Victorian bed had a hand-embroidered bedspread of cream and gold thread. The two prints of her favorite childhood pet dogs, Casper and Milton, hung on the walls.

He removed his jacket and threw it onto the Queen Anne chair, then shrugged off his boots and socks. After unbuttoning the cuffs on his shirt, he stood in front of her and took her hands in his. He pressed them to his chest. "Take it off me, Rebecca."

With trembling fingers, she began to unbutton his shirt. Starting at the top, she worked her way down one by one. Her mouth had gone incredibly dry. Occasionally, she would flick her gaze to his. The molten heat in his eyes as he stared at her mesmerized her like nothing she had known before. The intensity of the moment mounted as she finally freed the last of the buttons.

A small whimper escaped her lips as she pulled the shirt off his shoulders and removed it completely. His perfectly toned body now stood before her in all its glory. Each clearly defined muscle on his chest drew her attention. The rise and fall of his breathing equaled her own. *All I have to do...* She reached out then and touched his bare flesh.

His skin felt warm and the muscles beneath honed. Her fingers drifted over him, feeling each delicious ripple of his taut body. The well-defined pectorals. The washboard stomach. With every stroke of her fingers, she felt him respond to her touch. Desire pooled in her stomach. She had never wanted any man as much as she wanted Jed.

Suddenly, he stopped the movements of her hands with his own. "Now it's my turn." His voice deep, his eyes dark and probing, as he stared at her.

Slowly, he undid the tie on her robe then peeled it back. It dropped to the floor, revealing her pale blue nightdress. Her hardened nipples showed through the silk material, aching to be touched. Her breasts heaved in anticipation as he slipped the thin straps from her shoulders, and it, too, pooled at her feet.

The window was open, and the cool night air feathered across her body, heightening her feeling of letting go. His gaze caressed her bare flesh. "I knew you would be perfect."

He pulled her into his embrace, his one hand winding into her hair, the other hand slowly travelling down her body. He kissed her lips as he circled her breast with his work-roughened hand. He tweaked the nipple with his finger and thumb until she moaned against his mouth.

He maneuvered her to the bed and slowly pressed her down onto it, covering her with his body. Drifting her fingers over his face, she took in every masculine detail. The high cheekbones, the strong jaw now covered with stubble. She liked the way it rasped against her skin. Smoothing over his manly brow ridges, she threaded her hand into his hair. The soft locks spilled pleasingly through her fingers.

When she looked into his eyes, she believed a hunger existed that only the joining of their bodies would quench.

"You're so perfect, Rebecca. I could eat you alive."

He feathered tiny kisses down her torso. His tongue lashed against her nipples, tasting, teasing, and biting the dark pink areolas as she writhed with pleasure. His mouth drifted over her skin. When he moved lower, he forcefully pushed her legs apart, his thumbs spreading her neatly trimmed pussy wide open to his gaze. "Jed, no." When his tongue lashed over her clitoris, she arched into the exquisite feeling. Jason had never done that.

He did it again, this time more forcefully, lashing and sucking at the same time. "Becky, you taste so good." A warm glow spread through her. He'd called her Becky. No one had ever called her that before.

His tongue licked her entire slit, circling her clit with long, sweeping movements. It was all she could do to keep breathing. Her hands fisted in his hair. He speared one then two fingers deep inside her pussy, penetrating her with a possessive authority.

Then it started, a heavy pressure building, rolling, and surging forth. The delicious intensity overwhelmed and consumed her until she finally cried out in ecstasy as her orgasm crashed through. She'd never had an orgasm before. Jed had literally taken her breath away.

She lay on the bed completely calm as he moved from her and began to shed the rest of his clothes. He smiled at her. "Now you look a bit more relaxed, honey."

"I am. Thank you, Jed. That was my first orgasm with a man." Her voice cracked with emotion.

"I figured as much, Becky. I'm real pleased it was me that gave it to you."

Overwhelmed with emotional feeling, she wiped a teardrop from her eye. The idea that she had been frigid had made her deliberately turn away from men. Yet, Jed had ripped that notion from her head in less than five minutes. For that she would be eternally grateful.

Now her body thrummed with a newfound sexual desire. It demanded fulfillment in the most carnal way possible.

When he was completely naked, her gaze drifted over him. He was everything she wanted in a man and more. He had a powerful physique from long days working a ranch. His body was broad with strong muscular thighs and biceps to die for. The breath seized in her throat at the size of his fully erect cock glistening with pre-cum. She shook her head. He was so large.

"Jed…I don't think…"

He smiled as he saw her worried stare. "Don't you worry none, Becky. I'll help you."

He knelt on the bed then ripped a condom from its foil packet with his teeth. He began rolling it down his shaft. He looked at her, his eyes dark pools. "Normally I'd ask you to do this, but I just don't trust myself. I don't want to shoot my load just yet."

Then he lay between her legs and stroked his hand into her hair. He kissed her lips. "I've wanted to do this for weeks."

"Me too."

"I know, all those furtive looks. You've practically turned me into an insomniac."

She laughed. "Then you shall sleep well tonight."

He shook his head. "I don't think we'll be doin' any sleeping, Becky. In fact, you can count on it."

His sheathed, hard cock pressed against her vagina. He covered her mouth with his, and she moaned against his lips as the head of his penis penetrated her. He waited a moment then pushed himself farther inside her, inch by slow, deliberate inch, pausing each time until he was seated fully to the hilt. Stretched beyond belief, she savored the delicious feelings running through her.

"Are you okay?" he asked.

When she nodded, he began to slowly withdraw and then press back inside her again. With his weight channeled down his powerful arms, he rose above her, strong and incredibly virile. The lamplight carved out his muscular body in fine detail, showing his well-defined muscles to perfection.

"Jed." She stared into his eyes.

He thrust into her. "You like that?"

Oh, God, he felt so big. Nerve endings she never knew she had came alive, demanding fulfillment.

He thrust again, only harder this time, making her body arch like a bowstring. She gripped onto his powerful shoulders, digging her nails into the taut sinews as they flexed with every movement he made.

He thrust again and smiled as she moaned with pleasure. He kissed her neck, biting her earlobe, then whispered, "Turns you on, don't it? My hard cock deep inside you."

A moan tore from her lips. His words, coarse and basic, ignited a fire inside her. A fire that would not go out until she had given herself to him completely. "Oh, Jed. I want…" Her voice trailed away as he thrust once more deep inside her.

"I'm gonna fuck you till you've come, and then when you think you can't take any more, I'm gonna fuck you again."

Jed talking dirty turned her on far more than she could ever have imagined. Arching into the exquisite feeling, she pressed against him, wanting everything that he could give her. Feverishly, she kissed his lips, tasting his mouth with her tongue, exploring his body with her hands.

She wrapped her legs around him and squeezed his buttocks, pulling him harder inside her.

"Say it, Becky. Say what you need."

"Oh, Jed, harder, please." She had never felt more alive as a woman. Each stroke of his cock rubbing against the inner muscles of her vagina brought her untold pleasure. Each penetrating thrust deeper than she thought possible. It felt like he was inside her womb.

He raised the tempo. "Yeah, we're like two peas in a pod. You like it fast and hard just like me."

"Jed, please. Jed, that feels so good. Please, Jed."

Then it began, and the pressure built, rising up from deep inside her, building in power, until it pushed her to the very edge of reason. Staring into his eyes, her mouth opened in surprise at the power and ferocity of her climax as it shattered inside her. The intensity of the sexual sensations coursing through her, made it impossible to think straight.

Her whole body tightened around his thick length. Her stomach muscles quivered and contracted as her pussy clamped and milked his cock repeatedly.

With barely a pause, he continued thrusting through the aftershocks, taking her further and further into ecstasy. In delirium she moaned out his name, "Jed, oh, Jed," she whimpered as he repeatedly pumped his huge cock inside her. Finally, when she thought she would faint, he came, erupting deep inside her aching pussy with a loud, satisfied growl.

Chapter Six

Sweat pooled between them as he lay on top of her, their breathing still labored. He smiled as he looked at her and stroked his hand into her hair. When she'd let her defenses down, the passionate woman had emerged. His instinct had been totally right.

Whispering those primitive words had really turned her on. The best of both worlds occurred to him. A true lady by day and a pure, sexy vamp by night.

When he could finally catch his breath, he withdrew from her, discarded the condom, and pulled her into his arms. She nestled snugly on his shoulder. "Are you okay, Becky?" he murmured, kissing her forehead.

She sighed. "Never more so. Another first for me."

"Yeah, that guy you dated must have been a real loser."

She giggled. "Yes, one of the finest. I guess now I can't play the prim English teacher with you anymore."

He chuckled. "Nope. I guess you can't." He lifted her chin and looked at her. Her cheeks were flushed pink, her eyelids all droopy. He'd never seen a woman look so satisfied. "I kinda like the fact that you come across all demure. Your hidden depths will be our little secret."

"Mmm, for your eyes only, Jed."

"Mmm, even better." He smiled and stroked his hand over her shoulder. "This feels good."

"What? My skin?"

"Of course, but what I mean is, lying with a woman feels so natural. Looking after Annie since she was born means I rarely get the chance."

"Yes, it must have been difficult."

"It was. Marlene died shortly after giving birth to her. There was an unforeseen complication." He rubbed a hand into his hair. "I suppose I'm over it now. Though I've noticed that Annie becomes more and more like her mother with each passing day. We were childhood sweethearts, you see. Got married when we were just kids ourselves. I'm just glad we didn't start a family right away, otherwise I wouldn't have had those years with her."

Her hand feathered over his chest, and he clasped it in his, aware that he had opened up to Rebecca more than he thought possible. Usually when he lay with a woman, he'd just keep the conversation on small talk.

He realized there was something different about Rebecca. Possibly it was her ability to listen without comment, or the fact that they'd spent time together while she gave Annie some extra schooling. Whatever the reason, he liked her all the more.

"Say, Rebecca, have you got any condoms here?"

Her head lifted sharply off his shoulder, and she stared at him. "Now why would you think I'd have any? There's hardly been a battalion of men knocking at my door."

He looked down into her beautiful face. "That's too bad, and I was feeling real horny." He let out a sigh. "Guess we'll just have to make do with the other four I brought with me."

The startled expression on her face made him burst out laughing. "You're so easily shocked." He touched her nose playfully. "I'm gonna enjoy teasing you."

"I might have known you were joking."

He flipped her onto her back and kissed her leisurely on the lips. He trailed a hand over her perfect breasts. "Who said I was joking?"

* * * *

"Well done, Annie. You've recited that passage beautifully." Rebecca saw how the praise encouraged her as the little girl beamed with pride.

"Why thank you, Miss Wade. I tried extra hard to get it right."

Stifling a yawn, she gave Annie her next task. Right now she needed sleep desperately. In all her life she had never felt so tired and satiated at the same time.

Jed had made love to her until the early hours of the morning when he had finally left to see to his ranch.

The man certainly had stamina. Her cheeks flushed with heat as she thought about some of the positions he'd had her in. Missionary seemed very tame now.

The most memorable moment during the night had been when she'd knelt on the bed, her hands gripping tightly to the brass headboard, while he'd taken her roughly from behind, fast and hard. With his one hand on her breast, his other hand had ministered to her needs, gently pleasuring her clitoris.

It was basic, like two animals copulating out of instinct, but she had never felt more desirable in her life. Jed made her feel more of a woman last night than she'd ever thought possible.

Unable to focus, she began to clean the board, only looking up when she heard a car draw up outside the schoolhouse.

Her heart slammed into her chest when she saw Jed ease out of the driver's seat. She had an incredible urge to run to him and fling herself into his arms.

Instead she watched as Annie jumped from her seat and hurled herself at him.

"Did you miss me, Pumpkin?"

"Sure I did, Pappy. Grandma told me to tell you that I'm growing like a weed and need some new clothes."

"Did she now?" He set her down and looked at her with such love that Rebecca knew he was thinking about her mother. "Yep, I guess she's right. Better go shopping before your pants turn into shorts."

Annie giggled, and he ruffled her hair. "Now run along to the car, Annie. I've just gotta speak with Miss Wade."

"Bye, Miss Wade."

Rebecca smiled. "Bye, Annie. See you tomorrow."

When they were left alone, Jed looked at her, and her heart skipped a beat. His heated gaze caressed slowly over her. Her whole body responded to him as though he had touched her.

He pulled her away from the windows, and then shook his head. "Nope."

"What do you mean, 'nope'?" she asked, enjoying the contact as he pressed her firmly against the wall.

"Just thought I might see a difference, Miss Wade, that's all. Every hair in perfect place." He leaned in, his hot breath fanning against her neck. "The sex kitten I unleashed last night doesn't show at all."

"For your eyes only, remember?"

He trailed kisses up to her ear and whispered, "It gives me the horn, knowing what you're really like."

"Jed," she admonished, beginning to feel the heat pooling into her panties.

He chuckled and pulled her hand to his groin. "There's nothing wrong in saying how you feel, Miss Wade." Her fingers smoothed over the bulge in his jeans. She closed her eyes, secretly wishing it was Sunday, and he'd be able to do with her as he pleased.

He nibbled her ear. "I wanna know how Miss Wade feels."

She shook her head, a smile beginning to form on her lips. He just couldn't stop teasing her. "Not here."

"I won't leave until you tell me."

"You make me—you make me go wet."

He nuzzled into her neck and whispered, "What's wet, Rebecca?"

A little strangled noise escaped her mouth. This felt so naughty and just a little erotic. Biting her bottom lip, she finally plucked up the courage. "You make my pussy go wet, Jed."

He smiled at her coyness. "See, that didn't hurt, did it? And said in such a refined English accent makes my cock real hard." He lifted her skirt, his fingers smoothing up her inner thigh until he reached her panties. The breath seized in her throat in a short, sharp gasp as he slid a finger inside her.

"Jed." Her pussy felt soaking wet as he circled her clit.

"I'd like to fuck you up against this wall right now, but I can't. So how about you come up to my ranch this Sunday? I can show you around, and then I can service both our needs."

She closed her eyes as the mental image began tormenting her. How she wanted him to do just that. He teased his finger over her clit until she whimpered. "Okay, just go before anyone finds you with your hand up my skirt."

He removed his hand and hungrily sucked her juices from his fingers. He kissed her cheek. "Now I hope you feel as frustrated as me."

* * * *

Rebecca couldn't believe how long a whole week lasted. Finally Sunday had arrived. Jed had told her that they'd go horseback riding when he showed her his ranch. So that was why she had chosen to wear a pair of jeans and a white blouse. He'd also asked her to stay the night, so she'd packed a few essentials into a small tote bag.

Her stomach coiled into a tight knot of anticipation as the sign for the Monroe Ranch announced her arrival. It was only when the track went on for some time that she realized he owned an enormous spread. Running the ranch must take up most of his time, and yet he'd go over to her house once a week to keep his side of the bargain.

Maybe she'd have a word with him about that. He'd done more than enough work on her house already.

Eventually, the drive opened out into a clearing, and a large, gabled ranch house with a deep veranda came into view. Trees circled the plot, casting leafy shade from the hot summer sun. Opposite the house was a huge paddock where two saddled horses were tethered to a fence.

When she stepped from her car, Jed appeared, a relaxed expression on his face as he sauntered across to her.

He kissed her briefly, a teasing smile to his lips as his gaze flittered over her face. "I've been looking forward to this all week, Miss Wade."

"Me too."

"Good." He pressed her back against her car and kissed her more forcefully, his tongue doing delicious things to her mouth. "Now, what I'd really like to do is haul you straight up to my bedroom, but it's such a fine day, I'll show you around first, and when we come back, there'll be no stopping me."

Rebecca could think of nowhere else she'd rather be, but she smiled and said, "You've got big ranch here, Jed. I hadn't realized. It must take up a lot of your time."

"Takes a bit of juggling, what with Annie, but I manage okay. Besides, 'round these parts, this ranch is considered quite small."

She giggled. "I forget Texas is huge."

"Well, how about I show you a bit of it right now?" He took her hand in his and began leading her over to the two tethered horses. "You said you could ride."

"When I was young, I went riding all the time."

"Now this one's yours. Let me introduce you to Pandora. She's a fine filly. She'll give you no trouble at all."

Rebecca ran her hand over the mare's head. Two lovely, big brown eyes stared at her. "She's cute."

Jed patted the large black stallion standing beside Pandora. "And this is Prince. He's my favorite, though he can be a bit temperamental."

Within minutes, they were on their way down a small dirt track and into the open countryside. Rebecca couldn't help but notice Jed's fine physique as he sat astride his horse. His long, powerful legs effortlessly controlled Prince. One hand held the reins, the other rested on his thigh. His broad shoulders commanded her gaze.

He grinned when he caught her staring at him. "Like what you see?"

"Of course," she replied huskily. She more than liked, she positively yearned for him.

"Who'd have thought the prim schoolteacher would have such lust in her eyes?"

"Does it show?"

He laughed. "No, but I just wanted to know what you were thinking."

Her cheeks flushed pink. "Oh, Jed, you're such a tease." She moved Pandora closer to him and tapped him playfully on his arm.

A devilish grin appeared on his face. "You're gonna get into some serious hot water if you carry on like that."

Her stomach quivered as she looked at him. He made her feel carefree. "Good. I can see I'm going to have to watch every word I say to you in the future."

When they reached the end of the track, the terrain changed, becoming flatter with fewer trees. "Come on, Becky, I'll race you to that oak over there."

"I think I should have a head start since Pandora here is smaller than Prince."

"Very well—"

Before he finished speaking, she took off on Pandora. This was so much fun. The wind whipped into her hair and lifted her hat to hang around her neck. The sound of Pandora's pounding hooves on the hard ground, music to her ears. Her own heart beat a rhythm that made her feel totally alive.

With two hundred yards to go, Jed gained on her. Prince at full gallop would be hard to beat, but Pandora held her own as she gave her the reins. Eventually, they'd almost reached the tree, and they both came to an abrupt halt in a cloud of dust.

Jed dismounted and tied Prince to a nearby bush, and she followed suit. They were both laughing.

Immediately, he pulled her into his arms and pressed her back against the tree. "Now what we have here is a prize cheat. No need to look the innocent with me. In these parts, cheats are dealt with severely."

Chapter Seven

Jed leaned in and kissed her smiling face. Rebecca exuded something he couldn't quite put his finger on. No matter, it would come to him soon.

"Now for your punishment."

In one swift movement, he held her hands above her head with one large hand and began tickling her with the other. She shrieked with laughter and tried to squirm away from his grasp, but he pressed his body more firmly against her, thwarting her escape.

Unable to catch her breath, her eyes began to water.

"What have you got to say for yourself?"

She tried to speak, but words wouldn't come.

"Well?"

"Jed, no," she gasped as he continued to administer her punishment.

"Is that an apology?" He grinned.

"No, yes. Stop—I can't stand being tickled." Her eyes closed tightly shut.

He relented then and playfully admonished her. "Damn it, woman, you are a cheat. The daughter of a clergyman, and on a Sunday, too."

"Yes, I know. It's outrageous, and it's all your fault for leading me astray."

"Mmm, I like leading you astray."

"Since meeting you I've learned how to let go. Jed, you've taught me how to live and enjoy life."

"Pleasure's been all mine, darlin'." Threading his hands into her hair, he released the pins from the tight coil she kept it in and watched in satisfaction as it cascaded around her shoulders. "Now you must always wear your hair down for me. You're the sexiest woman alive." Her raven black hair shone with a blue sheen from the harsh noonday sun, and her pale blue eyes sparkled from her perfect heart-shaped face. Surely Rebecca was the most beautiful woman he had ever seen? When he lowered his mouth to hers, she kissed him back with a promise that spurred his primal urge into action.

Her arms wrapped around him, her fingers combing into his hair as he pressed her forcefully back against the tree. He wanted to possess every inch of her, in every single way imaginable.

His cock hardened and strained painfully inside his jeans. When he heard her whimper of frustration, he nuzzled down to her earlobe and whispered, "I feel just the same way, darlin'. Now take off your jeans and panties. I need to be inside you."

He pulled her hand to his groin. "Feel how hard my cock is for you, Becky."

Already he could sense the effect his words and actions had on her breathing. The pulse in her neck beat noticeably faster.

He enjoyed turning her on. She was a woman that needed the verbal stimulus, too. Her previous lover just couldn't cut it.

Her cheeks flushed pink just the way he liked. She stared up at him and smiled coyly. "If you want them off, then you'll have to do it yourself."

Slightly surprised by her challenge, he nibbled at her earlobe. He felt the slight tremors that ran through her body. He knew then that she had pushed past her comfort zone, perhaps searching for the sexual excitement he had unleashed in her last weekend.

"Becky, you sure know how to turn me on." He slipped his hands into the waistband of her jeans, enjoying the slight gasp that broke from her parted lips as his fingers grazed against her bare skin.

He made quick work of her button and zipper. Then he knelt on the ground, removed her boots, and yanked them from her legs. He looked up into her face as he slipped the panties from her. Her eyes never left his as she stepped from them.

There was no rush. Still kneeling, he pushed her back against the tree then spread her legs wider with his hands. Opening up her pussy lips with his thumbs, he lashed his tongue over her clitoris. Her moan of appreciation told him he'd hit the right spot. This was something to be savored. The hotter the woman, the hotter the sex.

"Mmm, so wet for me, Becky. Just like at the schoolhouse."

"Oh, Jed."

Her eyes were closed, the dark lashes curling down onto her cheeks. Her waist-length hair blew slightly in the breeze. He sucked hungrily on her clitoris, driving his tongue deep into her pussy until she moaned out loud in pleasure.

When he pushed his fingers into her silken warmth, his cock ached to replace them. "Tell me what you want, Becky."

"I want you, Jed."

He teased her some more. "Exactly, tell me exactly."

"I need you inside me, Jed."

His cock was so hard now. Just one more sexy answer, and then he wouldn't be able to hold back any longer.

"Exactly, Becky. I wanna know exactly."

"Fuck me, Jed, please. Be rough with me." Her hands kneaded into his shoulders. Unleashed from her tight control her body arched into his.

* * * *

When he stepped from her, she saw the dark desire evident in his eyes.

"Now you're ready for me," he murmured gruffly as he undid his jeans and purposefully pulled them down.

Her whole body trembled with need. These feelings had been missing most of her life. Yet, Jed had teased them so easily from her.

All she wanted, all she could focus on, was her own sexual gratification.

Her pulse rate increased as she saw his erect cock spring free. The head glistened with his arousal. He rolled a condom down its huge length then roughly undid the buttons on her blouse. His work-roughened hands grazed against her skin as he yanked it partway down her arms. The front-fastening bra seemed to satisfy him as he unclasped it and allowed her breasts to bounce free.

He lifted her by the waist, and she braced her hands on his shoulders as she wrapped her legs around him. The bark bit into her back as he pressed her firmly against the tree. "You don't know how fucking sexy you look," he drawled as his cock pushed against her moist entrance.

He entered her then with an urgency she found thrilling. Stretched apart, she panted for breath as he seated himself to the hilt. Then he moved his arms under her legs and braced his hands under her buttocks.

With her thighs resting over his biceps, he began thrusting inside her. She had never felt so wanton in her life. Her legs spread wide open in invitation. Her breasts naked, accepting, as his tongue lashed slowly over them. The hot sun soaked into her bare skin. Surely this was the most wicked and indulgent thing she had ever done?

She ran her hands through his sun-streaked hair, savoring the texture against her fingertips. Her own needs took control, and she yanked on his hair, forcing him to kiss her. When their tongues met, desire pooled and pulsed around his cock.

Nothing had felt this raw and sexual before. She braced her arms on a convenient branch, relieving some of her weight. He thrust even deeper then, making her moan against his mouth. Slowing the moment, he kissed her so sensuously, his huge cock impaling her so fully, that every nerve ending throbbed with desire.

Held, suspended over him, she stared into his eyes as her pussy tightened deliciously around his thick length. "Oh, Jed."

"Come for me, Becky. You're so close, I can feel it." He kissed her lips as he ground himself hard into her. Just that one movement sent the nerve endings in her clitoris into overload. An orgasm so powerful and beautiful ripped through her body, making her reassess just how great sex could be with the right man. Her stomach contracted and quivered, driving a huge convulsion around his cock. More ripples flowed, pulsing over his huge shaft inside her, making her moan against his mouth.

He gripped her tighter and thrust more urgently inside her, passing through the aftershocks, building the momentum once more, over and over until she climaxed again. Her whimpers of satisfaction loudly filled the air around them. With a loud guttural groan, he came, spurting his cum deep inside her. Spent and exhausted, he rested his forehead against her naked breasts, and she stroked her hand tenderly through his hair.

Surely this intense feeling that happened between them was more than just sex? It felt like they'd shared a lifetime together already, but then maybe to Jed, this was all normal.

When his breathing had slowed, he lifted his head and looked deep into her eyes. "You're one hell of a woman, Becky, and no mistake."

* * * *

As Jed laid the blanket on the ground, he couldn't help but study Rebecca. There was no doubt about it. The woman had simply taken his breath away. As he glanced at her buttoning up her blouse, she looked like butter wouldn't melt in her mouth. All that was left was a faint blush to her cheeks. Now he knew different. Poised on the edge of orgasm, he'd felt the tight sheath of her body contracting around him. Her moans of passion had spurred him on, making him drive deeper inside her until they'd both come at the same time.

Sex with Rebecca had taken on a whole new meaning, but what that was, he hadn't a clue. He knew he wanted her now more than ever.

"Come over here, Becky. I'll give your shoulders a rub."

She sat down in front of him, and he began rubbing his fingers into her flesh. "Mmm, that's wonderful." She lifted her hair out of the way.

He leaned forward and caressed her neck with his lips. "So, what did you think of your first outdoor adventure?"

She smiled coyly at him. "Who said it was my first?"

He doubted she'd done anything like that before, so he called her bluff. "Well?"

"I think actions speak louder than words, Jed."

He chuckled. He'd been right. "They do indeed." He held out his arms. "Come." Then he rolled onto his back and pulled her to rest on his shoulder. "Now what I'd like to know is why you don't go to church on Sunday?" He placed his hat low over his eyes to shield them from the blazing sun.

"Well I can't see you beating a path to God's door, either."

He smiled. "Well I've only ever stepped inside a church four times. One time was filled with joy, and the others filled with sadness. What's your excuse?"

"It's complicated. Maybe I'm not a good person." She broke off a piece of grass and began twirling it between her fingers.

"If you'd rather not talk about it, just say."

"No, I'm fine. My father ran a local parish in Hampshire, a rural county just outside London. To everyone in that parish, he was the epitome of goodness and light. He could do no wrong. Only I saw a different side to him. One that I learned to despise and hate.

"I was an only child, you see. Mother died when I was six years old. Maybe that was the cause of his violent mood swings. He certainly hated the sight of me and would do anything to ruin my self-confidence.

"In the end, I tired of his constant character assassination and tried to leave, but I was weak and gave in to him. I stayed because he'd become frail. I thought it was my destiny to remain single, so when he approved of Jason, it seemed the perfect solution."

"So, in a way, you went out with Jason in order to make your father like you?"

She stared at him. "Do you know, I think you're right. I never really cared for Jason in any meaningful way. I could have saved us both a lot of heartache if I'd stood up to my father from the very beginning."

"Rebecca, in retrospect, we would all do things differently. Hell, I've made loads of mistakes over the years that I'd change given a second chance."

She gently placed a finger to his lips. "I spent years listening to the pulpit sermons that my father gave, and yet he never acted remotely Christian to me. That's the real reason why I don't go to church on Sunday. I'm all sermoned out."

"And rightly so by the sounds of it. Rebecca, do you look like your mother?

"Yes, I do look like her."

"The reason I ask is, I know how I felt when Marlene died shortly after giving birth to Annie. The resentment had been there, even if only for the first few days. In the end, I found Annie to be the greatest comfort I could possibly have." He could remember it as though it was yesterday. The grief and loss had overwhelmed him. He couldn't even bear to look at Annie. In the end, it was Marlene's own mother who had placed the tiny bundle in his hands. From then on he knew he'd be all right.

She touched his hand. "Marlene left you a very precious gift. A part of herself."

He breathed in and rubbed a hand over his face. On occasions the past would rise to the surface, and this was one of them. He'd never been one to show emotion, but he felt so at ease with Rebecca that he just couldn't help it. "How beautifully put, Rebecca." He turned and looked at her lying against his shoulder. Her pale complexion appeared flawless and her eyes sincere. "You're a good person, and you don't have to go to church to prove it, either."

Then he kissed her tenderly on the lips. This just felt so right, lying in the grass, the birds twittering in the trees. The sun soaked into his very being, making him feel so very alive.

"Now how about we stay here a while, then we can go back to the ranch, and I'll cook us up a fine steak meal?"

"Mmm, sounds like heaven."

"That's the answer I was hoping for, darlin'."

Chapter Eight

Two months later

Rebecca marveled at how fast the weeks had flown by. Her relationship with Jed had grown in intensity. She was very attached to him now. In fact, truth be known, she loved him. Although he'd voiced nothing about how he felt about her, so she had kept these feelings to herself.

Over the weeks she had learned nearly everything about him. His likes and dislikes, of which there were many. The way he liked his toast buttered when hot, the strength of the coffee she poured first thing in the morning. These all gave her an insight into the man.

Only last week, she'd gone to his ranch and watched him rope young steer calves in order to tag them for the first time. His actions had been so masculine and manly, and yet he handled her with a tenderness that sometimes overwhelmed her. He saw to her every need as a woman.

Although that wasn't to say he was like that all the time. Oh, no, there were times when he seemed to stare right through her. On these occasions when they had sex, he would be like a man possessed, pounding into her until they both climaxed in pools of sweat.

She parked the car at Jed's ranch, and smiled as he approached.

"Now you're a sight for sore eyes, and no mistake," he murmured, kissing her on the lips.

"You too, Jed." He literally took her breath away with his fine physique and masculine scent. "A week seems an awful long time."

Now that the school holidays had begun, she didn't even get to see him when he would pick Annie up from school.

He cleared his throat. "There's been a change of plan. Annie's grandmother's not well, so she hasn't gone over there to stay."

Since the beginning of their affair, they'd deliberately kept it from Annie. It had been her idea, and perfectly acceptable given the circumstances. Why involve his daughter? Surely, if their relationship floundered, wouldn't it confuse her even more given that she was her teacher? Jed had agreed this was the best option open to them. Besides, Annie wouldn't be adverse at spinning a few yarns of her own in order to impress her friends.

As disappointment settled in her stomach, she said, "That's okay, Jed. I can come back next week."

"Now that's the exact reason why I didn't call. Annie will be fine. It's not as if she doesn't know you, is it?"

"As her teacher, Jed, but not as your lover. How did you explain it to her?"

"I just said we'd become good friends, and that you always stay over on Sunday night."

"When did you tell her that?"

"This morning."

"That's hardly giving her time to adjust, Jed. You don't realize that she'll view me with suspicion. Now I'm someone who can threaten her relationship with you."

Rebecca knew all about the jealousies of children, having witnessed plenty herself when her father's parishioners would come seeking his advice over an unruly stepson or stepdaughter.

"I think you're exaggerating, Rebecca. Annie's just a kid. Besides," he took hold of her arm and began escorting her into the house, "I insist."

Annie sat at the kitchen table. An assortment of paper and pencils scattered around her. She looked up as they both entered the room. "Hi, Miss Wade, Pappy said you were coming over."

"Hi, yourself, Annie," she said cheerfully.

* * * *

Later, Rebecca relaxed back into the comfortable old leather couch in the open-plan living area and reflected on the day's events. On the whole, it had gone remarkably well. All three of them had enjoyed a lovely horseback ride around Jed's land. He'd proudly shown her the new perimeter fencing he'd just started to install along the eastern edge.

Although with Annie vying for her father's attention every moment of the day, it had been hard for them to have their normal, open relationship. They had to keep strictly to protocol. A warm glow had spread through her on several occasions when she'd seen him look longingly at her.

In an hour or so, Annie would go to bed, and then she and Jed could finally be on their own. She guessed this was what all parents were doing the whole world over, waiting for the kids to go to bed in order to have a little bit of time together.

Annie sat on some scattered cushions in the middle of the floor, and as Rebecca studied her she saw, perhaps for the first time, the beautiful young woman she was yet to become. Her clothes, her hair, all said tomboy, but maybe she just hadn't had anyone show her girlie things before.

"Have you ever braided your hair, Annie?"

Annie looked at her and shook her head. "No, Miss Wade."

Rebecca smiled. "I can show you. Would you like that?"

"I sure would, Miss Wade. Pappy says my Momma used to braid her hair, but I don't rightly know how to do it." She went over to the large oak dresser and removed a framed photo along with a brush. She handed them to her. "That's my Momma. Ain't she pretty?"

Rebecca studied the photo. A very blonde and very pretty young woman smiled at her from across the years. She'd seen it several times, but Annie didn't know that. "She is, and I think you look just as pretty. Now let's see if we can braid up your hair the same way."

* * * *

When Jed returned with two coffees, he stopped in the doorway. The sight of Rebecca brushing Annie's hair arrested his movements. Surely this was what he'd always wanted, a happy family unit?

He took in the scene. Annie perched on a cushion, the framed photo of Marlene on the floor beside her. Rebecca calmly plaiting her hair.

He placed the coffees on the side table, noticing the little smile Rebecca gave him.

"Miss Wade says I'm as pretty as Momma."

"You sure are, Pumpkin. You look more and more like her every day." He'd known Marlene since they were both ten years old, and Annie looked the spitting image of her.

"Jed, have you any ribbons?"

He tried to lighten the mood. "What do you take me for, woman? When would I put ribbons in my hair?"

His daughter giggled. "Pappy, the ribbons are for me."

"Well, why didn't you say?" He scratched his head then went over to the dresser. He opened a drawer and pulled out a small bag. "Grandma sent these bobbly things over. Didn't rightly know what to do with 'em." He handed them to Rebecca.

She tut-tutted and shook her head, playfully saying to Annie, "It's a man thing." They both burst into laughter.

He sat down just as Rebecca secured the final plait. "There, all done."

"Thank you, Miss Wade." Annie stood and quickly turned to him, seeking his approval. "What do you think, Pappy?"

He felt his heart constrict. Suddenly she looked more grown up than ever. "You look real beautiful, Pumpkin."

Rebecca leaned back into the sofa. He put his arm around her and gently caressed the nape of her neck with his fingers. She smiled warmly at him.

Annie jumped on the sofa, squeezing in between them both. He moved his hand and placed it on top of her head. "Now it's way past your bedtime. It's time you took the nine o'clock walk, honey."

"Oh, Pappy. Do I have to?"

"Yes, you do. Now scoot. I'll come up in ten minutes to tuck you in."

Reluctantly, she rose and headed for the door. "Now don't forget to say goodnight to our guest."

"Goodnight, Miss Wade." Her big brown eyes looked at him. "Pappy, I don't feel well."

"You'll be all right. Now go to bed."

He watched her leave the room, her head down. He turned to Rebecca. "I don't usually have any trouble." Rebecca just smiled at him, and he asked, "Do you know something I don't?"

"I think Annie is a very clever girl."

He pulled her into his arms and kissed her possessively on the lips, delving his tongue into her mouth. He needed so very much to take her to bed and lay his naked body over hers. "I've wanted to kiss you properly all day."

"Me too."

Chapter Nine

Finally, Jed closed the door of his bedroom and turned the key. It was just past eleven in the evening, and they'd both had a shower.

He touched her lips as he pulled her toward the bed. "Now let's see how quiet you can be," he whispered, beginning to open the silk robe that she wore.

Wearing just a pair of black sweatpants, he sat on the bed. Still standing, she nestled perfectly between his legs.

"I'm always quiet," she whispered back. With Annie just down the hallway, they felt like a couple of naughty teenagers.

He grinned at her. "Uh-huh, Becky, your passionate cries really turn me on, but you'll have to keep them well and truly hidden tonight."

As if to make a point, he peeled her robe back and suckled hard on her naked breast. She gasped and bit her bottom lip to stop herself from moaning out loud.

He chuckled and lay back on the bed, pulling her on top of him. The hard contours of his warm, naked torso pressed against her bare breasts.

"Well, I don't know what you're looking so smug about, Mr. Fancy Pants Monroe. You'll have to slow down your usual tempo because this brass bed squeaks every time you move."

He stroked his hands through her hair and kissed her lips, his gaze flicking from her mouth to her eyes. "Becky, this is gonna be pure torture, making love so quietly."

The heat from his body burned into her as she lay on top of him. She stroked her hand down to his groin and caressed her fingers over his hard penis.

"It could take hours, Jed." She grazed her lips against his. "All those slow movements, until you'll finally be able to release your cum inside me." When she saw the look of frustration on his face, she giggled into his shoulder. Since being with Jed, she had become quite practiced in talking more provocatively. It felt natural with him.

He slid his hands down to her buttocks and smoothed them over her bare flesh. "I just love your cute ass." Then he hooked his legs around hers and held them fast against him. "Mmm, now I've got you exactly where I want you." His one hand trailed into her buttock cleft and rubbed into her pussy. The other hand fingered her puckered hole.

Unable to move, she bucked with the contact. She whimpered against his chest. "Jed, that's so sensitive, I won't be able to keep quiet for much longer."

He chuckled. "One day soon, I'm gonna claim this ass as mine." The thought of something so deliciously forbidden sent a thrill running through her, and her stomach muscles quivered at the thought. No more repressed English schoolteacher for her.

"Mmm, I can feel that turns you on as much as it does me." Then he let her go and rolled her onto her back.

He smiled into her eyes and opened his mouth, ready to speak, when the door handle to the bedroom started to turn.

"Pappy, why did you lock the door?" Annie's frantic voice called out.

He looked slightly apologetic as he went to see to his daughter. When he opened it, he said, "I always lock it."

"You do?"

"Of course, now what's wrong, Annie?"

She flung herself into him and started crying. "Oh, Pappy, I don't feel too well."

"Come on, let's get you back to bed."

Rebecca wondered how much her presence had caused Annie's unusual malaise. When he returned, she asked, "Does she have a temperature?" Surely she had to give Annie the benefit of the doubt.

"I don't think so."

"Do you have a thermometer? I can check her out if you like. A sort of second opinion."

"Would you?" He held her hand and smiled. "I know today has been a bit of a disaster, but I'll make it up to you."

"I'll hold you to that." She kissed him on the cheek.

"Let me get the thermometer."

* * * *

When Rebecca came back into the bedroom five minutes later, she was smiling.

"I think she'll be all right, Jed. She doesn't have a temperature, and I know the perfect cure for what's affecting Annie."

When she began putting her clothes back on, he asked, "What are you doing?"

"I'm implementing the cure. Within a half hour, Annie will be as right as rain."

"You're leaving? Aren't you exaggerating?"

She touched his cheek with her hand. "Trust me, Jed. I think I know a little about what children are capable of. After all, I work with them every day."

"Maybe, but you don't have to leave."

"Jed, if I stay, I'm afraid Annie will make it impossible for us to be together."

"I don't think Annie is that manipulative."

"Jed, we've just dropped a bombshell on her. She really needed to be eased into this situation, if at all."

"What do you mean, if at all?"

"Look," she took a deep breath and stared directly at him, "why involve Annie, especially if you don't want to take things any further?"

Feeling as though he'd been backed into a corner, he said, rather sternly, "Now who's being manipulative? You've turned this whole episode to your advantage. Well let me tell you something, Rebecca. Don't try pinning me down about our future together because I don't make snap decisions. Especially when they involve my daughter."

He saw the hurt on her face, but it was too late. The words were out of his mouth before he had time to think them through clearly.

"I see. Then it's just as well I'm leaving. I'll see you around, Jed." With that, she turned on her heels and began walking down the stairs.

He followed her and grabbed her upper arm just as she went to open the front door. "If you go, don't bother coming back." Now why on earth had he said that?

She stared at his hand grasped tightly around her, and he immediately let her go. Her cool eyes warned him. "Haven't you got someone to look after?" Then she left without a backward glance.

He thumped the wall in frustration. Now why hadn't he apologized? He knew Rebecca meant a great deal to him already. So why not just come out and say it? He ran his fingers through his hair in frustration.

When he went to check on Annie, she was tucked up snugly with all her dolls. Her hair was still in the braids. He stroked his hand over her head. "These dolls have more of the bed than you."

"Has Miss Wade gone?"

"Yes, Pumpkin, Rebecca's gone back to her own home. Why?"

"Well, she told me that she must be coming down with the same illness as me. Only…"

His daughter paused, and he prompted, "Go on."

"It's just that I feel fine now, Pappy. So she couldn't have had what I had."

He chuckled to himself as he left her room. Rebecca had been right. He just hadn't bargained on a possessive daughter. Now all he had to do was find a way to make it up to Rebecca.

Chapter Ten

After three days of ignoring the telephone, Rebecca finally gave in and answered it.

Jed's Texas drawl burst down the line. "Rebecca, what the hell are you playing at?"

"I don't know what you mean, Jed. Besides, if you're intent on having an argument, I'll put the phone down."

She heard his deep intake of breath. "Rebecca, we need to talk."

"Why?"

"You know why."

"Jed, you made everything perfectly clear on Sunday. What more is there to say?" He'd turned on her when she'd only been trying to help.

She heard the frustration lacing his voice as he continued, "Rebecca, I need…" When he paused, she could almost imagine him dragging a hand through his hair. "Look, this is no good. I'm coming over. Right now," he emphasized.

"Jed, it's not convenient."

"Well, that's just too bad, honey." She was left staring at the telephone as the line clicked dead.

It was just over an hour and a half before his SUV came to an abrupt halt on the drive.

Well, if he thought she'd rush to the door, he'd have another think coming.

Anyway, she needn't have worried. The mere sight of him as he stepped from the car arrested her movements. Dressed in jeans and a black denim shirt, he looked manlier than ever.

His thick, sun-bleached hair fell about his face. His piercing blue eyes moodily scanned her home. She stared at him through the kitchen window, unable to take her eyes from his, unable to deny the strong physical attraction between them.

He walked around to the kitchen door and tried the handle. Still she couldn't move. He braced a hand, either side of the doorframe, and stared directly at her through the glass window. Her stomach twisted into a tight knot at the intensity of his gaze. "Are you gonna open this door?"

"What for?"

"So we can talk."

"I don't feel like talking, Jed."

"I'm gonna count to five, and then you'll only have yourself to blame. One."

Rebecca pressed her body back against the wall, her gaze connected to his. No matter how angry she felt with him, the power of his presence affected her like nothing before. The fact that he was still here meant something, but she needed more proof.

"Two."

Her breathing increased as she braced herself. The coolness of the kitchen tiles permeated the blouse she wore. "Go away," she called, but she didn't really mean it. In her wildest fantasies, she imagined him breaking the glass, pulling her into his arms, and professing his undying love for her. Then making mad, passionate, unbridled love to her right here on the floor.

"Three. You're only making it worse for yourself."

There was no way he could break the door down. She'd just had it installed, along with several brand-new locks. She wondered what he'd do when he got to five.

"Four."

The blood pounded in her ears as she stared directly at him. Willing him to come in. Wanting him to consume her very being.

"Five."

Not knowing what to expect, she closed her eyes. She heard nothing but the deafening sound of silence.

Then, a loud crash took her by surprise, and her eyes flew wide open just as the kitchen door rocked back on its hinges.

"Rebecca, honey, I'm the big bad wolf, and I've come for you." His piercing blue eyes bore into her as he walked purposefully toward her. He was angry.

Unable to speak, she just stared back. The fact that he'd just kicked her door in had momentarily rendered her speechless.

* * * *

The atmosphere between them felt supercharged and ready to explode at any moment. When she'd refused to open the door, he only had two choices. Giving up just wasn't an option.

"How dare you," she whispered, raising her hands to strike against his broad chest as he stood in front of her.

He caught her wrists and held them firmly in his grasp. Rebecca had a temper to match his. "I dare." He pulled her into his embrace and roughly kissed her lips. "Now don't say anything. You're coming with me."

In one movement he hauled her over his shoulder and began carrying her up the stairs.

Held in a fireman's lift, she shouted out, "Let me go, Jed." Her fists pounded against his back.

"Not a chance in hell, lady." Then he swiftly thwacked her behind with one masterful stroke. That would make up for all the nights he'd lain awake trying to work out what he wanted.

The sharp slap to her backside made her yelp, and she stopped hitting him. "What was that for?"

"That's for not picking the telephone up for the last three days."

"Serves you right."

"Maybe, but not three days, Becky." He slapped her ass again…hard. All the trouble he'd gone to this afternoon, taking Annie over to her grandmother's and dropping her off. "I'm in no mood for making an apology. Now I'm gonna serve swift justice the way I see fit." They'd reached her bedroom, and he roughly threw her on the bed. "Now strip." He began shedding his own clothes, desperate to be inside her.

"Jed, you need a lesson in how to treat a woman."

He stared at her. "No, you're the one that needs the lesson, and I'm gonna give it to you fast and hard, just the way you like it."

Finally naked, he reached forward and dragged her toward him. "I thought I said strip."

"You want them off, you take them off," she taunted him. Her words only heightened his arousal, and he wrenched her skirt from her. He quickly relieved her of her panties, ruining them as he tore them from her body. The sound of the material shredding echoed around the room.

"To hell with this," he mumbled in frustration. With one rough movement, he started tearing at her blouse, ripping the buttons open. They pinged to the floor as he yanked the flimsy material from her. He did it so fast the sleeves tightened inside out on her arms, making it virtually impossible to remove. He pulled at her exposed bra, and the clasp gave way with a loud snap. He tossed it to the floor, a statement of his power over her.

He saw the effect his actions had on Rebecca. Her breasts heaved with excitement. Small whimpers escaped her mouth as each piece of clothing was unceremoniously discarded. "Jed, I can hardly move my arms."

"That's too bad, honey. I'm in charge. You'll have to live with it."

As she struggled to free her hands, he rolled a condom down his shaft.

"Jed, wait."

"No chance."

He knelt on the bed and lifted her to straddle on top of him. His hard cock pressed against her vagina. A moan tore from her lips as he buried himself to the hilt. Completely at his mercy, she stared into his eyes. Yeah, she liked him taking control. He began thrusting hard inside her. His one hand cupping her shapely ass, the other held against the nape of her neck. The warm, tight sheath of her body clasped firmly around his cock.

He kissed her breasts, suckling the pale pink tips until she arched into him.

"Now you've gotta promise me a few things, Becky."

"Yes, Jed." Completely dominated and all compliant, her voice had gone quiet, and she'd given up trying to remove the blouse.

"Never, ever stop talking to me again."

"Anything, Jed. I'm sorry I've been mean."

He leaned forward, pounding into her with deep, measured thrusts. He nuzzled into her neck and whispered in her ear, "I'm gonna fuck you so hard now, so you'll remember. And when you've come, I'm gonna fuck that cute little ass of yours, too."

He knew his words and actions sent her spiraling toward her climax. Her pupils dilated, and she spoke his name in soft, feminine whimpers. The kind of moans that teased his cock into spilling his seed, sooner rather than later.

When she finally freed a hand from her blouse, she wrapped her arms possessively around him, making him feel wanted and needed. Her fingers wound into his hair, and she arched her body into his just as her orgasm shattered through. The pulses contracted around him in tight waves. Her beauty at that moment took his breath away. Rebecca was everything he needed and wanted in a woman.

He stroked his hand through her hair as her breathing returned to normal. "Becky, look at me." Lifting her head, she stared into his eyes. He knew he could lose himself in those pale blue irises. "I'm sorry if I upset you on Sunday. You do mean a great deal to me, I love you, and I want us to be a family."

"Oh, Jed, I love you, too."

"I want us to get married, Becky. There's no one else I'd rather spend the rest of my life with." For the last three days, he'd done nothing but think about their relationship. They had the basis for a perfect family unit. They had all gotten along so well, just that slight glitch with Annie toward the end of the day. Even that could be overcome with time and patience.

She touched her hand to his face. "I love you, Jed. I fell for you the first day you came to my house." He smiled. The day she'd cured his bad neck. He kissed her lips, feeling that he'd finally found the perfect woman. Now he wanted to make her his permanently.

"Lie on your stomach, Becky."

Chapter Eleven

In a daze, Rebecca lay on her stomach. When Jed burst through the door, he'd taken her breath away. She'd never felt more desirable as he'd savagely ripped the clothes from her body. Then he'd made love to her with such intensity, staring into her eyes as he'd roughly taken her.

Now he'd asked her to marry him. She smiled, feeling totally at peace. Jed loved her. He actually loved her.

He began massaging her shoulders, working down her spine in bold, arcing sweeps. "Now this has to be done slowly." He gently rubbed the cheeks of her ass with his fingers, stroking them incredibly tenderly.

"Oh, Jed, that's so nice."

He chuckled. "We haven't even started yet, honey."

She heard him open a jar, and then he said, "Raise your butt for me."

Rebecca kneeled and rested her elbows on the mattress. Her pulse rate had increased dramatically. Doing something so taboo sent her breathing into overdrive.

"Rebecca, you don't know how sexy you look."

When a cold sensation touched her puckered hole, she gasped and tried to pull away. Jed held her firmly around the waist and administered the lotion, rubbing it around the rim. When he pushed a finger inside her ass, she whimpered. The sensation felt so alien, and yet so very erotic.

"Jed," she gasped.

"It's okay, honey. I need to help stretch you a little, so I don't hurt you."

More lube followed, and then he slid two fingers inside her. She felt so full. She couldn't imagine accommodating anything larger.

"How does that feel, honey?"

"It feels good, Jed, but so tight. I don't think…" Her words trailed away as he packed in yet more lube. This time he worked three fingers inside her tight ass.

Her heart rate increased as he knelt behind her. "You'll be fine," he promised as his cock rested against her most intimate of places.

Holding her breath, she waited as he pushed the head of his penis inside her ass. A sharp sensation caused her to gasp, and she squeezed the bedspread, twisting it between her fingers. Then Jed grasped tightly onto her hips and drove in the rest of his hard shaft.

"Oh, my God, Jed." The feeling felt so foreign and exotic. She had never felt so full.

He clasped her possessively around the waist. "Rebecca, you belong to me now."

"Yes, Jed." It felt like he'd branded her as his own. She whimpered as he slowly withdrew and thrust back in. After caressing her clit, he inserted his fingers deep into her pussy. The knowledge that he filled both holes at the same time sent her arching into his hand. "God, that's so…"

"You feel so good, Becky. I love you, do you hear me?" He held her more tightly, thrusting hard inside her once more.

"Oh, Jed, I love you so much."

Her whole world turned upside down. The feelings running through her ripped apart her preconceived ideas that she wouldn't enjoy it. Sweat trickled down between them. Her body tightened around his thick length. A tight coil of tension started in her stomach, twisting into a knot, then surged down into her womb, where the first ripples of her orgasm began to grow.

They feathered out, rising in intensity, until she shouted out as the most spectacular orgasm ripped her apart. Convulsions so exquisitely close to pain rippled around him, pulsing his shaft repeatedly until he, too, cried out as their ecstasy took hold. He came then in one giant surge, and a low animal growl tore from his lips as he spilled his seed deep inside her.

They rested together, still intimately joined, until their breathing returned to normal.

He stroked a hand through her hair. "Come on, let's take a shower together."

* * * *

"You okay, Becky?" he asked as they snuggled under the duvet. They'd made love once more in the shower and now lay exhausted in her bed. Her whole body glowed from his attention.

"It's just a lot to take in."

He pulled her more tightly into his embrace and began massaging her shoulders. When she rested her head against his chest, he wrapped his arms protectively around her.

"What do you need to know?"

"Everything."

He cupped her chin, and smiled warmly. "Rebecca, I love you and want to marry you."

To have a man like Jed made her feel like the luckiest woman alive. "Then how do you feel about having two women competing for your attention? You know it won't be easy."

"Now *that* I haven't begun to figure out. I just hadn't bargained on a possessive daughter. Within two minutes of you leaving, she was as right as rain."

"It's not really her fault. Annie hasn't had to share you with anyone for the last eight years. Although I'm sure we'll work it out in the end."

"You're very positive."

"I am." She wrapped her arms around him. "I have the love of a good man to make it all worthwhile."

"You have indeed, and I'm sorry about last Sunday. After you left I did a lot of thinking. I realized that what we have is very special."

"It is special, Jed." The connection they had with one another must be unique. No one else could feel what they had.

"Something like this only happens rarely, so we need to grab it with both hands."

She giggled. "Well you certainly did that when you burst through my kitchen door."

He chuckled. "I couldn't help it. You sure know how to wind me up, honey."

"I'll remember that in future." She stroked her hand along his cheek, her eyes focused on his. "Although it did have its compensations. Your caveman technique really turned me on."

"Me too."

"Thank you, Jed."

"What for?"

"For releasing me from the past. I'm finally the woman I always wanted to be."

He kissed her lips. "You're one passionate woman, Rebecca, and you're all mine."

Epilogue

Six months later

While Rebecca rinsed the dishes from their evening meal, she couldn't help but smile as she watched Annie and her father enjoy some time together. They were both laughing as Jed chased her around the garden with a water pistol.

They'd certainly all come a long way in the last six months. Each of them had learned some big lessons. Annie, who'd had the most to lose, had finally accepted Rebecca. It had taken a lot of patience, cajoling, and lots of girlie nights in, but eventually the tension had diminished.

When Annie started playing on her swing, Jed strolled back inside the ranch house. He came up behind her and wrapped his arms possessively around her waist. Rebecca closed her eyes, melting back into his embrace. She couldn't imagine a day without him now.

"Mmm, you smell good." He nuzzled her neck with tiny kisses. "Are you happy?"

"I am. Watching you both together makes me happy, Jed, especially as Annie seems so contented."

He turned her around and pressed her back against the sink. "To my way of thinking, we've all gained. Annie's gained a mother figure. You've gained—"

"A wonderful husband and stepdaughter. I hadn't thought of it like that, Jed." She touched his nose playfully. "So that means you've gained a wonderful wife."

He kissed her lips and smiled at her. "No, Rebecca, not just a wonderful wife. I've found the sexiest woman alive." He kissed her possessively. "And she's all mine."

THE END

www.janbowles.com

SIREN PUBLISHING *Classic*

JAN BOWLES

Cowboy Bad Boys 3

BOUND BY THE MONTANA MOUNTAIN MAN

BOUND BY THE MONTANA MOUNTAIN MAN

Cowboy Bad Boys 3

JAN BOWLES
Copyright © 2011

Chapter One

Cassie Philips checked the U-Haul trailer attached to the back of her Jeep and then eased into the driver's seat. Minneapolis lay three days behind her, and this was the final stretch of the journey to her new home in Whitewaters, Montana.

When her Uncle Seth had bequeathed her his ranch, it had been totally unexpected. As the only living relative left, the news had come at a rather dark time in her life.

A bitter divorce battle with Aaron had left her homeless and virtually penniless. Even now, she still couldn't believe he'd tossed aside their five-year marriage so easily. Up until then, she'd considered the marriage to be a happy one. She should have more rights. It had been Aaron, after all, who had committed adultery. Her lawyer had suggested that had there been children, then things might have been very different. The irony of that was not lost on her.

Her hand shook as she gently brushed the tears from her eyes. Just over a year ago she'd been blissfully happy. Pregnant, and with a husband whom she thought loved her, things couldn't get any better. Then she'd miscarried, and her happiness had suddenly come to an abrupt end.

Well, Minneapolis held far too many bad memories. Maybe Montana would help clear her mind. At just twenty-seven, she'd made up her mind, she would never, ever, trust a man again.

As she turned out of the motel parking lot onto Interstate 90 for the last time, she breathed in a sigh of relief. Tonight she would be in her very own home. Tomorrow would be the start of her new life.

* * * *

Brad Dawson closed the stable doors and looked once more at the old Philips' place. Already dark, that was the second time he'd seen flashes of light in the last ten minutes. It certainly looked odd. The place had been empty for a few months now.

He rubbed his hand into his hair. One part of him couldn't care less. He'd had a running feud with Seth Philips for the past ten years. Now the old coot was dead. So who cared if the place got ransacked?

The other side to him. The more neighborly side thought he ought to investigate. If there was someone stripping its contents, then surely he should report it to the local County Sheriff.

Well, it was no good thinking about it. He'd drive over there, park down the track, and see if he could catch the culprits red-handed.

* * * *

Cassie shone the beam of light once more inside the Jeep. At least she had a flashlight. She took the last of the groceries from the backseat. Arriving in the dark had not been the plan, but circumstances beyond her control, like that flat tire just outside Billings, left her little choice.

Tomorrow she'd deal with the utility company. Right now she just wanted to make up the bed and prepare something to eat.

Just as she closed the passenger door behind her, the bag was ripped from her hand, and she found herself unceremoniously pressed against the side of the Jeep. The breath literally rushed from her lungs. With the wind knocked from her, she became aware of two hundred pounds of male flesh pinning her fast.

Her instinct was to scream, but he held her so tight, her mouth lay crushed against the cool metal.

"Just what the fuck do you think you're doing?" A deep, masculine voice cut through the night air.

Tired, hungry, and more than a little pissed by the way the day had turned out, Cassie used all her previous experience of self-defense training and jabbed her assailant with an elbow. She managed to create just enough leverage to wrench her mouth free.

"Take your hands off me, dick brain. I live here. Just who the hell are you?"

"Fuck." Immediately, he stepped away from her. "I'm your neighbor, Brad Dawson. I live just across the way from you. I thought you were ransacking the place."

When Cassie shone the beam of light toward the voice, she caught a glimpse of a very tall man. At least six-foot-four. He blinked several times as the flashlight picked out his features. A strong jaw with those delicious masculine lines she always liked creased around his mouth. He looked about mid-thirties with dark brown wavy hair and gray eyes. The irises were so pale they almost looked silver in the harsh light.

He was broad too, filling out his tan leather jacket and jeans.

"I suppose you felt safe tackling a woman on her own."

"Well, you didn't look much like a woman in the dark. What with wearing a baseball cap an' all. It all looked mighty strange to me."

"That's just great. I'll wear a label next time." Cassie felt her hackles rise. This Neanderthal knuckle dragger thought she looked like a guy?

Probably feeling embarrassed, he ignored her curt remark. "Why not switch on the lights instead of scrabbling around in the dark with a flashlight?"

"Pardon me, Mr. Dawson. If that's all I had to do was flick a switch, don't you think I'd already have done it? The simple fact is the electric's not connected. Now if you'll excuse me, I've got to get on with moving in."

"Have you tried your generator?"

"I don't think I've got one."

"Everyone's got one 'round these parts. When winter comes, the power's often down."

She sighed. "Then I'll have to sort that out in the morning, too."

"Look, Miss, er, I'm afraid I don't know your name."

"Cassie Philips."

"Miss Philips, we seem to have got off on the wrong foot. As a neighborly gesture, and in place of an apology, I could look at that generator for you."

When Cassie lifted the bag of groceries off the floor, she knew straight away that the eggs inside had broken. Her retort couldn't have been more acerbic. "Best not, I think you've already done more than enough damage, don't you?" With that she turned and entered her home. Cassie knew her tiredness made her behave far ruder than normal, but she just couldn't help herself.

Within a few minutes, the lights suddenly came on. As she looked properly around her home for the first time, tears sprang into her eyes. What sort of a legacy was this? Paint peeled from the walls. A collection of old tins and bottles lay scattered around in every available space. Stacks of newspapers rose from the floor in various sized piles, taking up one corner of the room. Old dishes of moldy food still sat on the pine dresser and table where they had been left. Something scurried along the wooden shelving, and as she looked closer, several cockroaches were intent on evading the light. A small scream left her lips, and she shivered involuntarily. Had her uncle really lived like this? She shook her head. If this was the living room, she dreaded to think what the other rooms would be like.

* * * *

At least he'd gotten the generator working. Now he had something with which to salvage the evening. That was a lesson learned if anything. What was he thinking? Never get involved. Especially when you had neighbors named Philips. They both had impressive tongues.

As he stepped into her hallway he called out, "Miss Philips, I've fixed the generator. There's—" He stopped speaking as he came into the living room. What he saw simply took his breath away.

Cassie Philips had removed her baseball cap, and her long blonde hair flowed down past her waist. A perfect heart-shaped face with gorgeous, pouting lips looked at him through sultry baby blue eyes. How could he have mistaken her for a man?

"I know," she whispered. "Kinda makes you stand and stare, but I had no idea that Uncle Seth was a compulsive hoarder."

He cleared his throat and dragged his eyes from her, noticing for the first time the state the room was in. The place looked like a trash can.

He blew a whistle of surprise. "Old Seth was a real recluse. People 'round these parts always knew he wasn't the full measure. Guess he didn't like to throw anything away."

He could clearly see she was upset, and she wiped the tears from her eyes. "Is that the generator?" she asked, pointing to the electric light overhead.

He nodded. "You've got enough gas to last a month, so I suggest you get it topped off before winter comes."

"Well thanks, Mr. Dawson. Guess you came in handy after all. You'll have to excuse me. I've a lot of cleaning up to do."

For a moment, her vulnerability surfaced, and then it was gone. The cool mask was drawn neatly down to hide her feelings from him. He wondered what the hell she was doing here. Her perfect hair, perfect manicure, and perfect skin all said city girl. Montana in the winter was no place for a woman like her. He'd give her six months, tops. Then she'd sell and go back to wherever she came from.

Maybe then he'd be able to buy that piece of land that had eluded him these past ten years. Seth Philips had been adamant he couldn't have it, yet it stopped his business dead in its tracks. He just couldn't develop the ranch the way he wanted.

"If there's anything you need, Miss Philips, just ask. I live in the ranch a couple miles down the valley. You can't miss it."

* * * *

The very next morning, she looked around the property. The house was as she'd suspected last night, in total need of a makeover. Outside she could see her land stretching from the river, down to the road. In total she now owned about a hundred acres. Not an enormous lot, but large enough for what she wanted. Next to the house stood a large wooden barn filled to the rafters with bailed hay.

When her uncle had become ill, all the animals had been sold off. The barn would make a good place for rearing chickens. Maybe she'd get a goat, too. Her intention was to become self-sufficient. The less she had to rely on the outside world, the better.

Cassie spent the next three days raking out the rubbish. She had a fire going in the yard, and after sifting through the contents, most of it went up in flames.

She felt quite sad, destroying someone's life so quickly and easily, but she reasoned that her uncle hadn't always been so bizarre. As age had crept up on him, he had become increasingly mentally unstable. Her mother had told her great stories of when they had grown up together. It was just the later part of his life that he'd begun to hoard things.

Some noteworthy items she kept. A beautiful framed photograph of her uncle and her mother when they were children. There appeared to be several documents with her neighbor's details on them. It looked as though he was buying a piece of land from her uncle and the deal had fallen through.

Maybe she'd pay Brad Dawson a visit and see what he'd been proposing to do. At the moment, she was very low on cash. If she could make some money while still keeping a roof over her head, then all would be well and good.

Indeed, the house had been in such a state she'd immediately ordered a new bed and mattress and some paint. That had cut deep into her savings.

As she watched the flames consuming everything, she marveled at how little she'd thought about Aaron.

Aaron and his new wife were just a distant memory. She looked up at the surrounding mountains and breathed in the fresh rarefied air. This was simply beautiful beyond words. Coming to Montana had been the best thing she'd ever done.

As Cassie threw the last of the rubbish on the fire, she caught a glimpse of a horse and rider fast approaching. Brad Dawson slowed down as he brought the horse to a controlled halt and dismounted right in front of her.

Having lived in the city most of her life, this new mode of transport made her heart somersault. He looked like he'd just stepped off a movie set, with his jeans, denim shirt, and black cowboy hat. His eyes twinkled in the sunlight as he looked at her.

"Just thought I'd stop by and see how my new neighbor's doing."

"I'm fine. Finally cleared the house out, as you can see. Broke one or two nails in the process, but they'll grow again."

He nodded, his eyes flicking from her face to her hands and back again. "That's too bad." Just why had she shown him her hands? She really couldn't care less about her nails breaking. Maybe deep down, she wanted him to know just how hard she'd worked. But why the need to impress him? Then he said, "I should warn you that the winters get pretty harsh here."

"Meaning?"

"Nothing. Just that you should get stocked up real early."

"I intend to." She felt he had something more on his mind. "Is there anything else you wish to say, Mr. Dawson?"

"Maybe you should think of selling, that's all. Save you a lot of heartache in the long run. It gets real cold up here as the nights close in. It's not a place for a woman like you."

Cassie felt indignant. Whenever she was in his presence, she just bristled. "And what sort of woman would that be?"

"City girl." His eyes pierced into her.

"You sure have some audacity, Mr. Dawson. Maybe you should just mind your own business. I don't think men are the only ones who can cope in a harsh environment. I came from Minneapolis, and we had pretty severe winters there, too."

He laughed out loud. He removed his hat and thwacked it against his leg. "Hell, sweetheart. Winters in Minneapolis ain't nothin' compared to what we get here. You get four inches of snow in a day. We get four feet."

Folding her arms across her chest, she fixed him in her gaze. "If I were to sell, I suppose you know someone who'd most likely buy it."

"Maybe." A half smile formed, deepening the creases around his mouth. What was it with dimples, anyway?

"Like you, perhaps?" When he didn't answer, she continued, "I found those documents you drafted up. Maybe that's why you want me to sell. Perhaps you're not really interested in my welfare, after all, but in that piece of land you want to get your hands on."

He placed his hat back on his head. "Whoa now, lady, slow down. I assure you that was the last thing on my mind."

"Mr. Dawson, I was going to come and see you in a day or two and discuss that parcel of land. But I think my Uncle Seth was a good judge of character. He could tell at a glance that you were up to no good. I've no doubt you only offered him a fraction of what the land is worth, thinking he was too old and crazy to understand." She pointed the one manicured finger she had left at him. "So no, Mr. Dawson. I won't be moving, and I won't be selling, either."

He smiled as he studied her. "You'll learn." He mounted his horse and then turned to looked at her as he gathered the reins in his hand. "Don't say I didn't warn you." Then he rode away as calmly as anything, leaving Cassie wondering if she'd imagined the whole episode.

She stormed into the house. If there was one thing she hated about a man, it was pig-headed chauvinism. Well, she had news for him. Cassie Phillips would show him she could handle anything Mother Nature could throw at her, and then some.

* * * *

As Brad rode away, he couldn't help but smile. The woman had spunk, that was for sure. She was a little firebrand. Okay, so he may have been thinking about that piece of land, but he wanted to warn her about the harsh winters, too. Make her think a little about planning ahead.

Her face had been smudged with soot, and she looked kind of cute with her hair in braids. There was something very earthy about her, which was unusual considering she was a city girl. Though she wasn't his usual type, but then he didn't really have a type. At thirty-five, he'd had more than his fair share of women. He just hadn't found one he wanted to spend the rest of his life with. Cassie intrigued him. He wondered just what a woman like her was doing in a place like this, all on her own.

Chapter Two

With the nights drawing in ever more quickly, Cassie decided to pay a visit to the local town of Whitewaters. After stocking up on all the essentials, she stopped at a local hardware store she'd spotted on the drive in.

The female assistant behind the counter greeted her. "Hi, sweetie, how can I help you today?"

Cassie smiled. The woman looked about the same age as her, but with chestnut shoulder-length hair and brown eyes. Although her makeup had been heavily applied, she was quite pretty and tall. She wore a skirt that Cassie would normally describe as a large belt and a low cut cream top. The buttons of which were half undone, revealing her well-developed cleavage. The sort that would make men look twice.

"I recently moved into the area, and I was wondering if you could advise me on any essentials I might need. I've been told the winters here are pretty harsh."

The woman sprang into life. "Well, now, sweetie, you've come to the right place." The shop assistant paused as she studied Cassie. "Say, would you happen to be the lady who moved into ol' Seth's place?"

"Yes, that's me." She held out her hand. "Cassie Philips."

"I'm Joleyn. Everyone knows me around here," she said, taking her hand in response. "Say, do you have a shovel?"

Cassie shook her head.

"Well, you're gonna need to carry one in your car at all times. You may have to dig your way out of a snowdrift, if it gets too deep.

Now have you got a survival pack?" As she pulled one off the shelf, her skirt rose even higher. Cassie imagined the men of Whitewaters would take a strong interest in this lady.

Placing the pack on the counter, she continued, "If you get trapped in your car, you just shimmy inside this. It will keep you nice and warm, may save your life." She pondered for a moment, placing her index finger to her glossy lips. "Hmm, let me see, snow chains, you got any?"

"No."

"That your Jeep out there?"

Cassie nodded, and a set of chains found their way onto the counter. As she looked at the mounting supplies, Cassie wondered just how much all of this would cost. Then she reminded herself these were essential. If she were going to stay, then that's what she had to have.

Joleyn continued, "Have you met the Mountain Man yet?"

She shook her head. "Mountain Man? No, I don't think so."

Joleyn giggled. "He's called that 'round these parts because he takes serious guided treks into the mountains. Knows them like the back of his hand. Surely you must have met him. He's your neighbor, Brad Dawson?" It was said nonchalantly, but Cassie had the sneaking suspicion that the woman was eager to know all the gossip.

"Yes, briefly. Why?"

"Well, you watch out there, sweetie. You might just become another one of his conquests. He's practically roped every woman in the valley into his bed. Trouble is he don't stay long enough to get to know 'em."

"Is that so?" The more she found out about Brad Dawson, the more she disapproved of him. Though the name Mountain Man had certainly piqued her interest. It made him seem far more rugged and dangerous.

"Yeah, Brad roped me, too."

"You went out with Brad?" Cassie studied her a little more closely. So that was Brad's type. With all respect to Joleyn, Brad seemed to like the more obvious kind of woman.

"Just one look at those eyes. Well you know how it can be, sweetie. He sure has a way with words. I've been between Brad's sheets on more than one occasion. As have all the other girls 'round these parts." Joleyn giggled. "Brad and I split more than three years ago. Broke my heart at the time, but it's all for the best. I'm happily married now."

"I'm absolutely sure I'll not be one of his conquests."

Joleyn laughed. "Well, sweetie, someone who looks like you do will surely have piqued his interest. Especially as you live on your own in the ranch just down the way from him. The whole valley's been talking about you."

The bell rang as the door to the store opened, and she became vaguely aware of someone walking up behind her.

"Please don't worry on my account, Joleyn. I've met Brad Dawson, and I wasn't the least impressed with him."

"Afternoon, ladies."

As soon as she heard that male voice oozing with a deep, velvety bass, she knew it was him. Why hadn't Joleyn warned her Brad had just entered the store? The woman looked at her briefly, a smug smile to her face. Cassie knew she'd done it on purpose when she purred, "Afternoon, Brad." She then leaned on the counter, her full breasts virtually spilling from her skimpy blouse. "Sure is nice to see you again, sweetie."

Wearing a sheepskin jacket, jeans, and a black Stetson, Brad walked up to them, an amused expression on his face as he turned and studied Cassie.

Surely he'd heard everything she'd said about him. Feeling like she wanted the floor to swallow her up whole, she continued with her purchases. "I'll take them all, Joleyn. Thank you."

As she waited for her credit card to be accepted, she turned to him. He was still watching her. Her whole body responded to his presence. Her palms grew sweaty and warmth flooded her cheeks. Her legs trembled. Just why was she reacting this way? To cover her nervousness, she said, "Thought I'd take your advice, Mr. Dawson."

"That's good. Folks 'round here are full of advice, ain't they, Joleyn?" He didn't once take his eyes from hers.

"We tell it how it is, Brad. You know that," purred Joleyn.

He chuckled. "Trouble is, folks 'round these parts want to know everything. I'll give you another piece of advice, Cassie. Keep your personal life private."

"I intend to, Mr. Dawson. Very private." Although he was speaking to her, she knew he was warning Joleyn, too. So Joleyn hadn't exaggerated about their relationship.

Her credit card was finally accepted, and she breathed a sigh of relief. Now she could finally take her purchases and leave.

"Thank you for your help, Joleyn."

"You're welcome, sweetie."

"I'll come back for the snow chains in a minute."

"I'll bring them." Brad began to collect them off the counter.

"No it's—"

"I insist." He turned toward her. His steely gaze allowing no argument as he looked at her. It seemed he'd made up his mind.

"Very well, as you wish." Grabbing hold of the shovel and the carrier bag, she rushed out the door.

He followed her outside and stowed the chains in the rear of her Jeep. "I seem to irritate you, Cassie. Why?"

"I've no idea, but you do. Perhaps I don't like being stared at."

He smiled, the creases forming around his mouth as he studied her once more. "Sometimes it's just nice to look at someone as beautiful as you."

Her head jerked up in surprise. "Flattery won't get you anywhere. I know all about you, Mr. Dawson."

"You know nothing about me, Cassie. Don't take any notice of what Joleyn has to say. She's just pissed because she married a drunk."

"My God, is there anything you don't know about each other?"

He laughed. "This is Whitewaters, Montana, Cassie. Everyone knows everyone."

"Then let me enlighten you. I've just had a very acrimonious divorce. I'm not looking for a relationship, ever."

He smiled, his silver gaze scanning her from head to toe. "Who said anything about a relationship? I just said I liked looking at you."

Feeling totally overwhelmed by his masculine presence, she pushed past him. He hadn't mentioned a relationship, had he? So why had she?

"You are the most irritating man I've ever come across." She yanked the door of the Jeep open and slid quickly inside, anything to escape this man.

His last words filtered through before she drove away. "Forever is a long time, Cassie."

* * * *

Brad watched her reverse the Jeep out the parking bay and onto the road. She sure looked spooked.

That was one part of the puzzle completed. Now he knew why she'd settled all alone, far away from her roots. Whatever her ex had done, he'd sure ruined her trust in men.

Still, the chase was all part of the fun. It was something he'd always enjoyed, and if it was too easy, then what was the point?

Mmm, Cassie Philips sure turned him on. He felt his cock harden in his jeans just thinking about her.

Now he'd have to use all his charm and guile to get her between the sheets, just like he'd done with every other girl from around these parts.

All he had to do was make her want him, as much as he wanted her.

* * * *

One month later

The first heavy snow had fallen over night, and winter had arrived with a vengeance. After seeing to her chickens in the barn and stoking up the fires, there really wasn't anything left for her to do.

As a web designer back in Minneapolis, Cassie had always been busy. If she didn't start working soon, she'd go stir crazy. She'd already put out feelers to do freelance work, and some projects had started to come her way.

What she desperately needed was an injection of cash. The sooner it happened, the better she'd feel. All of her thoughts kept coming back to that piece of land Brad Dawson wanted so badly.

Maybe she should just put aside her preconceived notions of the man and ask him what he wanted it for. If it seemed acceptable, then why not sell it to him?

There was no time like the present. She picked up the telephone receiver and dialed his number.

His rich, velvety voice made the hairs on the back of her neck stand up. *"Dawson Ranch."*

"Hi, it's Cassie Philips. Would it be convenient for me to come by this afternoon? There's something I need to discuss with you."

"Why sure, Cassie. I look forward to it. Shall we say about three."

"Yes, that sounds fine. You can expect me then."

When she put down the receiver, her hand shook. Just what was it with Brad Dawson, anyway?

* * * *

Brad looked at his watch again. It was almost four o'clock and Cassie still hadn't arrived.

His brow furrowed. She should be here by now, he reasoned, unless something had happened. He decided to telephone her. When the phone clicked onto the answer machine, he knew she'd already left.

He stepped outside and looked up the valley toward her ranch. He could just make out her red Jeep, a mere speck in the distance, no more than half way down her track. It was stationary. He chuckled to himself. The easterly winds had been blowing real strong all morning. She'd most likely got it stuck in a snowdrift.

Maybe he'd get Rufus out the stables and ride over there. See if she needed a hand.

The black stallion looked none too pleased as he began saddling him up. "I know it's cold out there, Rufus, but there's one thing I've learned about women. Help them out of a crisis, and they can't wait to share your bed." Rufus shook his head and snorted his agreement

A quick movement of his heels, and they were on their way. "Walk on, boy."

He half expected her car to start moving at any moment, but as he approached he saw the Jeep had gone into the drainage ditch at the side of the track. Cassie was nowhere to be seen.

The driver's door was open, and the constant pinging told him the keys were still in the ignition.

With a sense of urgency, he dismounted and removed the keys. The front of the Jeep was caved in. He was amazed that the air bag had not deployed after such a large impact. It looked like she'd left the track at some speed.

He re-mounted Rufus and began to follow a set of footprints in the snow leading back up the track. Then he spotted what looked like a bundle of clothes, lying in a snow bank.

Chapter Three

This didn't look good. When he got closer he could clearly see Cassie lying unconscious, half in a stream, half in the snow. He dismounted Rufus and moved toward her. He felt her pulse and breathed a sigh of relief. At least she was still alive.

Although by the color of her, she'd been in the freezing water and snow for some time. Her lips were blue, and her skin looked ashen and pale. On her forehead was a large gash. He guessed she'd hit her head on the car windshield, and then tried to stumble back to her ranch house before she'd collapsed.

He scooped her into his arms. My God, she was soaking wet and ice cold. Hypothermia had surely set in. Time was of the essence. She needed to warm up and fast.

He called, "Here, boy." Rufus dutifully trotted over. He managed to rest her over his shoulder and then ease himself into the saddle. After laying her across his lap, he headed toward her ranch.

As they rode up the frozen track, he kept calling her name. "Cassie, time to wake up now. Do you hear what I'm saying? I ain't asking, I'm telling you. You need to wake up right now, Cassie."

This did not look good. Not a flicker or murmur came from her. The sooner he got her inside, the better.

Eventually, he reached her ranch house. Thankful that he'd got her keys, he left her lying across Rufus and then opened the door.

When he pulled her onto his shoulder once more, he heard a small whimper escape her lips.

"Cassie, time to wake up now, baby." He felt her move slightly against him.

Her place couldn't have been more different from the last time he'd seen it. It literally shone like a new pin. She must have worked hard to create such a difference. He took her into the living room and laid her on the floor next to the roaring fire. Then, after tossing his sheepskin jacket aside, he went upstairs and pulled the duvet from her bed. He laid it on the floor next to her.

He felt the pulse in her neck. "Cassie, I gotta get these wet things off you." She murmured incoherently, but her eyes remained closed. Her lips weren't quite as blue, so that was a good sign. He pulled the sodden boots and socks from her feet. He knew it would be difficult to remove her wet clothing, so he took a seven-inch serrated hunting knife from his boot. "You are so gonna hate me, Cassie, and not just for ruining your clothes." Still, if she hated him afterward, then that meant she'd still be alive.

Brad was careful not to cut her baby soft skin, as the sharp knife made quick work of her jeans. He undid her belt, and then threw it into the corner of the room. He managed to shrug off her jacket then cut about four layers of clothing from her torso in one go. Slitting up the middle of her sweaters and then sliding the knife down through her sleeves.

His fingers couldn't help grazing against the naked flesh of her stomach and shoulders. A belly button ring sparkled from the firelight. Fuck, now that looked so sexy. Her body twitched slightly, but she still appeared unconscious. Her eyes closed, her lips slightly parted.

Down to just her bra and panties, he hesitated, and then felt the material. Wet through, too. Shit, if she didn't have the cutest, most fuckable body he'd ever seen.

"Damn it to hell, Cassie. Why do I have to be in this position?"

He quickly dispatched her red lacy underwear with the knife, its blade effortlessly slicing through the flimsy material. He cast the tattered fragments away. His gaze lingering briefly on her full, pert breasts, with their pale pink nipples, and her neatly trimmed pussy before he rolled her naked body onto the duvet and wrapped her in it. Her silken back and peachy ass his last view of her before he pulled the quilt tightly around her.

The feel of her skin against his only added to the mental torture. With a raging hard-on in his jeans, he felt guilty as hell. He felt like a voyeur taking advantage of her, but hell, she wasn't dead, and he would make damned sure she stayed that way. So he might as well enjoy the view. It would probably be the one and only time he'd get to see her naked. Why should he give a fuck if he was turned on? He was trying to save her life. Yet, all he could think of was the shape of her breasts, and the fact that she was a natural blonde.

"Brad, you are one motherfucker." He shook his head and chuckled slightly. "Yeah, well, when I stop looking, I guess I'll be six-feet-under."

He held her in his arms and began rubbing the duvet, trying to coax some heat into her skin. He patted her face with his hand. "Cassie, come on now. You need to wake up." Her forehead was cool to the touch, and he looked closely at the gash on her head. She'd taken one hell of a knock.

He heard her groan, and her eyes flickered open. Now that was a good sign. "Cassie, wake up."

Obviously in some discomfort, she began mumbling. Incoherent words at first. He stroked her hair. "It's okay, baby. You've hurt yourself, but you'll be all right."

"No," she whispered, shaking her head, a knot of tension in her brow. "Don't say that."

Still delirious, she began to sob.

Trying to give some comfort, he cradled her against him, and stroked her face. "You're fine, Cassie. You just need to wake up."

"But my baby's gone."

"Shh, now. Everything's fine."

"Just leave me alone, and go back to your floozy."

At first he thought she was talking to him, but he realized she was referring to her ex-husband. Her subconscious was dwelling on her most painful recent memories. It looked like the bastard had dumped her at a most vulnerable time in her life.

Suffering from concussion, she was just starting to come around. Now Cassie looked more stable he needed to get her some medical attention. He grabbed the telephone from its cradle and dialed the doctor.

* * * *

Initially, Cassie thought the voice talking on the telephone was Aaron's. Cocooned in a duvet, it seemed the most logical choice. The pain of loss filled her senses once more. Surely that was why Aaron was here? To comfort her because she'd lost her baby. Her head hurt so much it was difficult to think straight, but the voice didn't quite sound like Aaron's. It was deeper and more sensual.

Then it dawned on her. It was Brad Dawsons' voice, her neighbor. But what was he doing here?

"What happened?" she whispered, and then everything went black once more. When she came to, Brad was leaning over her. He looked all blurred. "My head hurts."

"Yeah, she's coming 'round now. Says her head hurts." He listened some more, and then said, "Okay, will do. Thanks, Doc. I'll keep her warm and safe until you get here." He put the phone down and caressed the side of her face. "You've had an accident, Cassie. Your Jeep ran off the road."

Somewhere in the back of her mind, the memory surfaced. She'd been going to visit Brad when she'd lost control. Everything from that point on was a blur.

So what had happened? How had she gotten here?

She watched Brad stoke up the fire, adding more logs. When she turned, she slowly became aware of her skin rubbing against the inside of the duvet. What the hell?

Quickly, she lifted the material and stared down at her naked body. Her head snapped toward Brad.

"Your clothes were all wet," he said matter-of-factly. His silver eyes unreadable as he stared back.

"You removed them all?" Her voice cracked with emotion. Brad, her neighbor, had seen her naked body. Stared at it and taken a keen interest in it, no doubt.

"Had to, Cassie, they were keeping you from warming up. Hypothermia had set in."

"You say."

"Your lips had turned blue."

"I don't believe this."

"That's up to you, Cassie. I did what I had to do."

"Like hell, you did what you wanted to do." A sharp pain seared into her skull, making her wince.

He rubbed a hand through his hair. "It wasn't like that."

"I bet you had a good look, though." When he didn't answer, she groaned and turned away. "You ain't no gentleman."

He chuckled. "Well I've news for you, Cassie. You ain't no gentleman, either."

"I'm so glad you're amused by it all."

"It's minus twenty out there, and I found you unconscious in the snow. It was the only option available."

"Now I'm humiliated beyond words, you can go. I don't need you anymore."

"I ain't leaving until the doctor arrives, whatever you think of me. You've had a nasty knock on your head, and he told me to stay with you until he arrives."

"How long will that be?"

"A couple of hours, the snow is pretty bad out there."

After a while, he moved her onto the sofa, and she slid in and out of consciousness. Eventually she awoke to find he'd made her some hot chicken soup.

Eating was the last thing on her mind. "I'm not hungry."

"You need to eat something warm. I know what's best for you."

"I see you're not big on patience."

He propped some pillows behind her head and made her more comfortable.

"Hmm." She clamped her mouth shut, refusing to eat anything.

"Very well, then I'll have to spoon feed you like a baby."

"You wouldn't."

"Try me."

He knelt at the side of the sofa and spooned some soup toward her. Glaring at him, she kept her mouth firmly shut.

"I see. So what's with this ex-husband of yours? What happened between you two to make you come all the way from Minneapolis to Whitewaters?"

Some things were just too plain hard to talk about, so she just shook her head, not fooled into opening her mouth.

"Let's see if we can do better." An amused expression formed on his face as he looked at her. "So when did you get your belly button pierced?"

Surprise made her open her mouth, and he spooned the soup inside before she could speak.

She swallowed. "Hey, that's unfair."

"I never said I'd play fair. Now one more."

She shook her head. Her gaze noticing the lines around his mouth deepening as he stared intently at her. Irritated that he found this all so amusing, she let her eyes wander over him. He'd rolled up the sleeves on his brushed cotton shirt, exposing the dark, masculine hair on his forearms. He certainly looked manly, with his broad shoulders and dark tousled hair.

Her eyes flicked to his. He was staring at her mouth, waiting for her to open up and take some more of the soup. For some reason, she duly obliged. If this was a test of wills, she knew he would win hands down. To her, it looked like Brad Dawson always got what he wanted.

When his silver irises connected with hers, it was as if he'd caressed her very soul. Those eyes had seen every part of her body, right down to the teensiest of her toes. If she didn't feel so shitty, she'd be as embarrassed as hell. Had he liked what he'd seen? From the way he was looking at her, she guessed he had.

"I suppose you always get what you want," she said indignantly.

"Yes, but this time I'm not so sure." His deep voice reverberated through her, sending tiny shivers up her spine. Bad as she felt, she knew he wasn't just talking about the soup.

"Oh?"

He studied her and opened his mouth. Then he turned and looked out of the window. "Doctor's here."

"Guess you're off the hook." She knew he was about to say something else.

He smiled at her. "Guess so." He leaned forward and kissed her lips, and God damn it, she kissed him back. "I'll let the doctor in on my way out."

Chapter Four

Just over a week had passed, and Cassie felt much better. As she toweled her hair dry, she looked in the bathroom mirror. The bruise on her forehead was beginning to diminish. However, the concussion had given her two very unsightly black eyes. Though they, too, were now beginning to fade.

The doctor had told her she'd had a lucky escape, and that Brad's quick thinking had undoubtedly saved her life. Indeed, he had pointed out to her how wet her clothes still were three hours after Brad had removed them. At the time, all she could think of were her ruined Dolce and Gabbana jeans and her expensive silk underwear. To top it all, he'd also seen her naked.

Now, with afterthought, she felt indebted to him. The least she could do was visit him and say thank you. This time, though, she decided to walk there. Better safe than sorry.

Truth be known, she couldn't wait to see him again. Night after night she had lain awake, unable to sleep, thinking about him. Imagining how it would feel with his hard body lying on top of hers. Fucking her slowly and deliberately, until she moaned out his name.

Going over there was her way of breaking the spell he'd put on her when he'd undressed her. All she had to do was look him in the eye, and this fantasy she had would simply disappear. His hold over her would be broken. Only then could she move on with her life.

That was the plan.

* * * *

When Brad saw Cassie walk through the gates of his ranch, he immediately felt a sense of satisfaction. So she didn't hate him, after all.

He watched her approach. Ankle deep in snow and wearing a sheepskin jacket, jeans, and knee-high boots, she walked up to him. Her blonde hair flowed from underneath a nifty black hat that kind of made her look cute. With a faint smile to her lips, she kept her eyes averted from his. He guessed she was embarrassed by what he knew about her.

What he'd love to do to that body of hers made his cock harden in his jeans. Thankful that he held a bag of logs in his hands to hide his obvious arousal, he smiled and showed her to the kitchen.

"It's good to see you, Cassie. Take a seat. I'll just get rid of these logs." He took them into the living room and dropped them by the open fireplace.

When he returned to her, she stood ramrod straight by the table. "Now they're a real nice pair of shiners. Who have you just done ten rounds with?" He joked to put her at her ease, but it didn't work, so he asked, "How do you feel?" He moved to the sink and began filling the coffeepot to keep his mind occupied. Her pouting lips were just so kissable.

"I feel fine, Brad. The reason I've come here, is to say thank you. If you hadn't acted so quickly, I don't think I'd be here to tell the tale. I'm afraid, at the time, I didn't appreciate what had happened."

"Cassie, I just did what I had to do." He noticed she still kept her gaze averted from his, just focusing somewhere on his shoulder. "And I'm sorry you've been put in an embarrassing situation." If she didn't stop chewing her bottom lip in that sexy way of hers, well, he'd fuck her on the table right here and now.

"I just feel awkward, I guess."

"Look, I'll pour us a coffee, and then we can discuss this some more. I can see you're upset by the whole episode."

* * * *

With his back to her, she watched him pour the coffee. He really did have a strong physique. His muscular body clearly outlined in the jeans and pale green sweatshirt he wore. The color of which only emphasized the impact of his silver gray eyes. Penetrating and precise, he seemed to watch her every move.

The spell had not been broken. God, how she wanted to be totally possessed by him. Fucked senseless by him. She couldn't even look him in the eye for fear he would know exactly what she was thinking.

When she had originally planned on coming over to thank him, she had hoped it would cure her obsession with him. Because he had saved her life, he now had an unusually strong hold over her. Brad knew every inch of her naked body. It made her blush, but it turned her on, too. Her panties were soaking wet at the mere thought of what she'd like him to do to her. He excited her like no man before. At the time, she had felt too ill to respond, but just looking in his eyes now simply took her breath away. The only way to function was to avert her gaze from his.

He placed the mug of coffee on the table. With him so close now, she nibbled on her lower lip. He cupped her chin and raised her face to his. Unable to look him in the eye, she focused on the creases at the side of his mouth. His masculine scent overwhelming her.

He spoke then, "Look at me, Cassie."

"I can't." Her heart hammered out an unfamiliar beat. She had never felt such strong sexual excitement before. She felt out of control, as he leaned in and brushed his lips against hers. The merest whisper of something more passionate to come, and she gasped in anticipation.

"Feel better?"

"A little," she whispered, licking her lips, wanting to taste the promise of him again.

He threaded his hand in her hair as he pressed her back against the table. His kiss this time more forceful and possessive. His tongue traced across her lips, tasting, teasing, and probing as he nibbled on her bottom lip. Pressed back against the table, his hips ground erotically into hers, the swelling of his hard cock pushing into the groove of her pussy. She moaned in appreciation.

"I want to fuck you, you know I do. And you want me to fuck you."

"I want you to make love to me."

"Is that all you want?" His eyes asking for further clarification.

"I want you to fuck me, Brad, so hard that I can't stop coming." There, she had said it. Her whole body quivered in excitement. There could be no misunderstanding. He was going to do it right now.

"Consider it done."

It had been a very long time since she'd last made love, and the feeling he aroused in her sent her hands winding into his hair. The texture and feel was soothing as it fell through her fingers. Placing her hands on his torso, she smoothed them up under his sweatshirt. The rippled skin of his chest felt warm and welcoming to her touch.

He pulled the hat from her head, and tossed it aside as she helped him ease his sweatshirt quickly over his head. Her gaze devoured the honed contours of his chest and abs. Their lips melded together as he began removing her coat. It, too, was discarded as she frantically sought the buckle of his jeans and pulled the belt through the loops, casting it provocatively aside. Undoing his zipper, she thrust her hand inside, and rubbed his engorged shaft with her fingers. This was something else. This felt more animal, and instinctive.

"You like that, don't you, baby? You like feeling my hard cock?"

"You know I do."

He smiled at her, his eyes twinkling. "Where would you like me to put it?"

"My pussy."

"Your wet pussy. Say the words."

"I'd like to feel your hard cock deep inside my wet pussy, Brad."

With a speed that surprised her, he pulled her sweaters over her head and let them drop to the floor. With his breathing as heavy as her own, she watched the rise and fall of his chest.

One part of her knew that the experience they'd shared had brought them closer together. The other part fully aware that he was probably using her, just like he'd used every other woman in the valley.

But she had needs, too. Her whole body felt on fire. Her desire had reached breaking point. When she had come to Montana, she had expected to live a single life, but she loved men too much for that. Maybe if she saw it as "neighbors-with-benefits", she wouldn't be too disappointed.

In reality, she didn't want a serious relationship with any man. Maybe something like this would be ideal. Just each of them servicing the other's needs without any commitment.

Desire pooled in her panties as she pressed her lips to his. He excited her like no other man ever had. He reached behind her and unclasped her bra. Then tossed it aside.

"Here." His voice rough as he pressed her down onto the table. He swiped the half-empty coffee mugs out of the way with broad sweeps of his arms. They smashed into small pieces as they made contact with the tiled floor.

"Yes," she gasped in excitement. Her legs spread open as his weight moved over her. The zippers of their jeans touched together in exquisite torture.

"You have the most spectacular breasts. So firm and full." He took a nipple into his mouth and suckled hard. His teeth nibbled at the sensitive flesh, until she gripped his shoulders more tightly and arched into him. "And so responsive, too." The areola had hardened into a tight nub, sending delicious pulses throughout her body.

Then he traced small kisses down her torso. His tongue snaked out to taste her navel adorned with an exquisite heart-shaped diamond.

"This is something else." He drew the belly ring into his mouth and suckled on it. "So sexy."

Brad placed her hands either side of the table, and said, "Hang on, don't let go until I say." Then he began undoing her jeans, a slight smile to his lips as she stared into his eyes. He quickly yanked them off along with her panties, discarding her boots in the process.

Standing before her, he pulled his own jeans down, revealing his cock. The size and width made her writhe in anticipation. The head engorged and dripping with pre-cum. "See, I'm ready for you, baby, but you're not quite ready for me.

"Open your legs," he whispered, his tone demanding her attention as he pushed his hand forcefully between them. As she opened them wider, his finger dipped into her wet pussy, sending powerful shock waves inside her. An intense moan escaped her lips as he circled her clit with his thumb and inserted two fingers into her moist channel.

Her head tipped back as she gripped the table tighter still. "Brad."

When he spread her pussy wide with his thumbs, she knew he was going to taste her. His tongue licked her slit until he drew her clitoris into his mouth and suckled hard. The exquisite sensation made her arch up, and she whimpered his name again. "Brad."

Rolling her engorged clit between his teeth and tongue, he pushed two fingers deep inside her pussy, curling them up against the inner wall. The pleasure mounted, and she arched off the table. A moan of appreciation tore from her lips. With the pressure at fever pitch, she felt herself tighten around his fingers, and her orgasm slammed through. Rolling in wave after delicious wave. "Oh my God, Brad. That feels so good." Her stomach muscles contracted, and her head thrashed from side to side, her climax so intense.

When he pulled away, she recognized raw intent in his eyes. "Now you're ready." With obvious sexual hunger, he lifted her legs and braced his cock against her moist entrance.

Wrapping her legs behind him, she tried to pull him inside her, but met with resistance. "Brad," she whimpered. "What are you waiting for? I need you inside me now."

"How much do you want my hard dick inside you?"

"I'm desperate for your cock, Brad. Do it now."

He smiled as her legs gripped him more tightly. This time he allowed her just an inch of penetration. Her lips parted at the feel of him, but she wanted more, and she squirmed toward him.

"Baby, are you satisfied yet?"

"No, I need more, Brad, more."

He leaned down and she bit her bottom lip, as he slowly sunk into her inch by slow, deliberate inch. A moan tore from her lips once he was seated to the hilt. He cupped her buttocks and lifted her ass from the table. With her weight channeled through her shoulders, her body arched automatically. Her breasts thrusting forward as she gripped the table for support.

Deliciously stretched, her gaze wandered down her body to his, noticing the fall and rise of her stomach from her rapidly beating heart and the way her belly ring caught the light. The sight of their intimately joined flesh as he began thrusting inside her caused her to moan out loud. This was so basic and exciting, watching his shaft slide repeatedly inside her. Time after time, until it glistened with her feminine juices. Each time he thrust his dick inside her pussy, her muscles clamped down on him.

When she looked into his eyes, her entire world fractured. The intensity in his gaze made her writhe in ecstasy. He'd been watching her the whole time. In this position he controlled everything, the pace, the amount of penetration. This was sex in its purest form. No caresses, no kisses, just a good, honest fucking.

Sweat trickled down his chest, catching in the dark, masculine hair. "Baby, you sure look sexy. Remember, keep hold of the table."

He slipped a finger against her anus. She bucked with the contact and moaned in protest. "No, Brad."

He chuckled. "Your asshole is just so cute. Don't worry, baby. I know you're gonna appreciate this."

When he pushed a finger inside her ass, her whole body convulsed into an intense spasm. Her pussy tightened around his cock, and her head tipped back as she arched into the feeling.

"That's it, baby, nearly there." Pleasure pulsed around him like never before. Her fingers gripped the table harder. "Come for me, Cassie."

The double penetration rocked her world. He thrust inside her repeatedly, each stroke deeper than the last. Filling her so completely, she thought she would lose her mind. Then another orgasm slammed into her. She writhed as each delicious ripple pulsed around his swollen shaft, making her shout out as it shattered around her.

"Fuck, Brad, that feels so…" Her lips remained slightly parted as her words trailed away.

Then he released her ass, lowering her to the table, and pressed his body over hers. His welcome warmth and weight pinning her fast against the hard oak wood. Brad thrust his thick length inside her once more, driving through the aftershocks. He grabbed her hands, and held them just above her head.

Staring into her eyes, he murmured gruffly, "Fuck, you feel good, woman." His hair had fallen down across his forehead. The channels either side of his mouth deepened as he smiled at her.

Then his lips sought hers, caressing over her mouth until he drove his tongue deep inside, mirroring the actions of his cock.

Completely possessed by him, she whimpered as he took what he needed, fast and hard. Her body slipped against the table as he thrust into her. He pushed her further toward ecstasy, until finally he spilled his hot seed deep inside her. She cried out once more, unable to comprehend that another orgasm had shattered through.

Chapter Five

Brad lay on his side, his one leg bent at the knee, as he trailed a hand down Cassie's naked back. He slowed down as he came to the delicious curve of her butt. She stirred awake, and he leaned in and whispered, "Cassie, much as I want to stay here, I've some chores to attend. I'll have to leave you here for a while."

Her eyes opened, and a faint smile flittered across her full lips. "Me too, Brad. My chickens won't be happy if I don't feed them soon."

"Not just yet." He pulled her into his arms.

Making love with Cassie had been just great. She'd been so responsive and unafraid to seek her own pleasure. Spread out and writhing on his kitchen table, he'd never seen any woman look sexier. Then they'd come upstairs to his bedroom, and they'd made love again. This time she'd knelt on the bed, and he'd taken her from behind, so he could feel her wonderful breasts as he pounded his meat into her.

As she snuggled against his chest, he wondered what she wanted from him. Did she want a relationship? She'd already told him she didn't, but what she said and what she meant could be two completely different things. He'd never taken any woman seriously before, but with Cassie, perhaps he'd make an exception. They certainly were on the same wavelength when it came to sex.

"So, Cassie, how do you want to handle this new relationship?"

"It's up to me?"

"Sure is, baby. If it was up to me, you'd stay over every single night of the week."

She giggled then raised her face to his, a serious look developing. "Look, Brad, I guess you know I recently divorced my husband. I'm afraid it was a very bitter separation." She sighed. "What I'm trying to say is I can't handle a heavy relationship right now. After what Aaron did, I don't think I can ever fully trust a man completely again."

"That bad, eh? So what did this asshole do to you?"

"He went off with my best friend, just when I needed them both."

He held her more tightly. She'd mumbled something to that effect when she'd been semi-conscious and delirious after her Jeep went off the road. Even something about losing a baby, but it would be unfair of him to bring that subject up now. If she wanted to tell him, then she would.

"Do you want to tell me any more?"

She shook her head. "It's still a bit raw. Best not, you might not like a sobbing version of me."

He kissed her forehead. "Tears don't scare me." He cupped her chin and angled her face to kiss her, tracing his thumb over her parted lips before slanting his mouth across hers. With her long blonde hair and baby blue eyes, she sure was a beautiful woman.

"Maybe we'll suit each other just fine. I know Joleyn told you plenty at the store. What I'm sure she didn't tell you is I'm okay with relationships. It's just when someone tries to force my hand. Trying to make me commit to them is a sure-fire way of ending it. When that happens, I guess I quite literally run for the hills. So now that we know where we both stand, it's your decision, baby."

She touched a finger to his mouth. "How about we see each other once a week?" She giggled as he raised an eyebrow. "Or maybe twice a week. Once at yours, and once at mine."

"Now you're talking a little more sense. The thought of making love in your bed really turns me on, Cassie. Of course, if you're feeling particularly horny, you can always just pop across for an extra session."

She giggled. "Mmm, a sort of neighbors-with-benefits relationship."

"Perfect." The idea sounded like heaven to him.

"The reason I popped across this morning wasn't for sex, though I must say it was an added bonus. I really came to thank you, and to ask you about that piece of land you wanted from my uncle."

"Oh, what do you want to know?"

"What you want it for?"

"There's a range of mountains on the other side of the valley that I want access to. At the moment, getting to them is out of the question when it takes over a day to divert around. If I had that piece of land, then I'd be able to get to them in a fraction of the time."

"Why?"

He playfully slapped her backside. "Look, let's get dressed, and I'll take you over there now. Show you exactly what I'm talking about."

* * * *

Brad retrieved most of her clothes from the kitchen, and she put them on, admiring his bedroom for the first time.

The giant bed, with its dark chocolate throw, and shaker style furniture complimented the walls of white and gold. It certainly looked relaxing, and not at all what she'd expected. Brad was certainly a man of surprises. She wondered what other hidden depths he had. There was no doubt he was a great lover. He'd taken her to heaven and back in just a few hours. She'd lost count of how many orgasms she'd had. Her whole body thrummed with a warm afterglow.

Now they'd had that talk, she felt better about their relationship, too. It seemed Brad didn't want to get serious, either. Well, that suited her just fine. After her divorce from Aaron, getting serious was the last thing on her mind. This way might just work for them.

She followed him into the kitchen, her gaze immediately drawn to the large oak table in the centre of the room. Images of their intimately joined bodies flashed through her mind. Her breathing automatically speeded up at the thought. Sex with Brad was something to be savored.

He caught her stare and smiled. "I don't suppose either of us will look at that table in the same way again."

"I'm just grateful it can't talk." Laughing, she shrugged on her coat and boots and found her hat resting against a jar of spaghetti where it had been tossed earlier.

"I've gotta feed the horses first. Then we can go over to your place."

Snow had just started falling again. The soft white blanket soaked up most of the sound around them as they walked across to the stables.

Inside, with steam rising from their coats, six horses stared back as he introduced them. He put more hay and food into their stalls. "This one is Rufus," he finally said, running his hand over the muzzle of a beautiful black stallion. "He helped me rescue you the other day."

Cassie stroked the fine-looking beast. "Thank you, Rufus. I guess I owe you one." It still felt strange that a whole chunk of her life had happened without her knowledge.

She followed him over to a barn, and he dragged out a snowmobile. "Best way to travel when the snow starts getting too deep."

He sat astride it and motioned her to sit behind him. "Now hold on tight. We don't want you falling in any more ditches."

After she wrapped her arms tightly around him, he fired the noisy engine into life. Clouds of smoke billowed from the exhaust. Then they were on their way, the snowmobiles' skis slicing effortlessly through the snow.

Eventually, they reached the edge of her land where a river separated it from his.

He stopped the engine. All they could hear was the sound of running water.

They dismounted, and he pointed to the river. "This is why I want this piece of land, Cassie. The river here is at its shallowest during the summer. I can cross it easily with my horses. You see, I take specialized expeditions into the unmapped part of the mountains. There are some wild tracks up there that I can really explore."

Suddenly she saw Brad in a whole new light. He seemed even more potent. She studied him more closely. The snow had now begun to settle in the brim of his black Stetson. The cut of his jaw just showed the early signs of stubble. The way he stood tall and manly, in the tan sheepskin jacket. Brad was a risk taker in the extreme.

"Isn't that kind of trekking dangerous?"

He smiled. "Sure is, baby, but I only take the most experienced adventurers. Novices need not apply. "

"Brad, I'll grant you the access."

"Thanks, Cassie, but I prefer to own the land because you never know what the future holds. I book expeditions up to a year in advance. If we fall out, or you sell the ranch, then that access could stop overnight. It would just ruin my reputation as a serious mountain guide."

"You saved my life, Brad. I'll give it to you." She could certainly see his point of view. He needed to be sure of ownership.

He stroked the side of her face. "That's very generous, but I'll pay you the going rate. That's if you'll sell it to me. I've had more than enough thanks with you just being in my bed. Besides, if we fell out, you would only end up despising me because you'd given it away."

"I know what you mean." Brad certainly talked sense. He seemed to be able to look ahead and judge a situation in its entirety. It probably came from his skills in assessing the risk from his guided treks. Nothing left to chance. "Okay, Brad, I'll sell it to you. I guess I could use the money."

"It won't make you rich, Cassie."

"I know it's not worth that much. It'll just tide me over until I get my freelancing properly set up."

"Ah, yes, I noticed you did web design when I was at your place the other day."

"Is there anything you don't know about me?"

He smiled and placed his hands on her shoulders. He looked into her eyes. "Guess I'm just someone who notices the details." He pulled her into his arms and delivered a kiss that left her breathless and wanting more. Never mind that they'd spent the last three hours in bed.

His hand slipped inside her coat. After unbuttoning her jeans, he rubbed a finger over her clit. Gasping for breath, she tried to pull away, but he held her fast. "Your fingers are ice cold, Brad."

He chuckled and slipped his finger deep inside her pussy. Nuzzling her forehead, he murmured seductively, "Don't you think the combination of heat and ice is very erotic?"

"Yes," she whimpered, barely able to stand upright.

"Well, when I come over to yours, I'm gonna bring a whole lot of ice, and a whole lot of heat."

The exquisite feeling felt tortuous and deliciously erotic. "I like the heat part, Brad, but not the ice part. I don't think I could stand it. You won't get me to stay still for long enough."

He nuzzled down to her ear, his voice deep and sensual. "That's what I thought. I'll just have to come up with a way to keep you in place, while I administer the pleasure."

"And what would that be?" Raising an eyebrow, she looked at him. A tight coil of desire centered low in her stomach as he gazed back.

"Mmm, that's part of the enjoyment, not knowing what's coming next."

The thought of Brad seeing to her every need made her arch her wet pussy into his hand. His other hand held her in a tight embrace as he kissed her possessively on the lips.

Standing in the middle of nowhere in such a tight embrace made her feel like they were the last two people alive. When the snow began falling harder, they made their way back to her place on the snowmobile.

He stilled the engine just outside the door to her ranch house. As she dismounted, he grabbed her hand and pulled her into his arms, and she rested on his knee. "So when do you want me to come over, baby?" His gaze caressed over her, a slight smile to his lips. When he looked at her like that, desire flared instantly within her.

"This Friday," she said breathlessly, already anticipating what would happen as soon as he arrived. Maybe she should at least show that she didn't just want sex. It would be nice to get to know him on a more personal level, too. "Come for dinner at around seven. I make a mean chili."

He nodded, the creases developing at the side of his mouth. "Make it a real hot one, then you'll enjoy being cooled down."

Chapter Six

When Friday arrived, Brad packed a small bag and headed over to Cassie's.

The day she moved to Whitewaters, he felt he'd been blessed. She was exactly the type of woman he'd been looking for. Beautiful, resourceful, sexy, and available, and above all, she wasn't looking for commitment.

Settling down had been the bane of all his previous relationships. None of his girlfriends had realized that by giving him an ultimatum. *It's marriage or nothing.* He'd always chosen nothing.

He liked the freedom his lifestyle provided. Sometimes he'd head out into the mountains and spend days under the stars. Having a wife and children would only interfere with that.

Grabbing a bottle of bourbon from the shelf, he headed outside to the white Dodge pickup.

When he reached her place, he drove straight into the open garage. He slid from the driver's seat and then knocked on her door.

Almost immediately, a vision of pure delight greeted him. Dressed in some tight black leather pants and a skimpy cream top, he could barely drag his eyes away from her full cleavage. With her blonde hair hanging loose, she smiled and ushered him inside.

"You look sexy as hell," he said, following her cute ass as she sashayed into the kitchen. He had to fight the sudden urge to bend her over the nearest chair and fuck her senseless. Instead he handed her the bottle of bourbon.

"Thanks. I haven't dressed up for ages. It makes a nice change."

He smiled. He felt sure she'd spent hours getting ready. It made him feel wanted and desired, and horny as fuck. He pulled her into his arms. "I've been looking forward to this all week."

"Me, too." Her husky reply as he kissed her full lips. His hands automatically splayed across her ass as he pulled her into his embrace. He squeezed her butt, dragging her against his hard cock.

She wound her hands around his neck and kissed him back. "I can't wait for you to take me to bed, Brad, but I insist we eat and talk first."

He grinned. Tonight was looking better and better.

"Baby, I'm hungry for whatever you've got."

* * * *

While Brad poured the bourbon, Cassie served their meal. She couldn't wait for Brad to take her to bed, but she was determined to hold out as long as possible. Surely this relationship wouldn't just hinge on sex. Besides, it had taken her all afternoon to finally settle on what to wear. She knew she'd chosen well when Brad couldn't take his eyes off her. Now she wanted to enjoy the moment for as long as possible.

"Any ice, Cassie?"

"Just a little," she said absently. "There's plenty in the freezer."

"That's good."

She just caught his smile as he pulled the bag of ice from the cool box and dropped two cubes in her glass.

His eyes flicked to hers as she just stared at him. "What?"

"I'm sure you've got something planned that involves ice."

"Whatever gave you that idea?" The dimples at the side of his mouth deepened as he put the bag back in the freezer.

Placing a finger to her lips in mock thought, she said, "Hmm, let me see." She pointed at him. "Why, you did."

"Wait and see. Half the fun is not knowing."

He was right. Already she could feel her pussy moisten in anticipation. Though she knew if Brad came anywhere near her with an ice cube, she'd run a mile.

"Anyway, let's eat."

They both sat down, and she raised her glass to his. "To newfound friendships."

He echoed her sentiment as their glasses clinked over the table. His eyes twinkled from the overhead lights. He certainly looked sexy in his dark gray shirt, and open collar. The neckline revealed a tantalizing amount of masculine body hair. He looked the maverick mountain man, all right.

Wondering how he viewed her, she asked, "Still think I'm a city girl?"

"No." He chuckled and began forking the chili to his mouth. He raised his eyes back to hers. "But, you look like a city girl tonight, with your spray-on leather pants. And I admit I did call you that shortly after I'd met you, but I've seen what you've done with this place. You're obviously determined to make a go of it."

"I am, Brad. Maybe it's thanks to you that I've done so well."

He raised his brows. "Oh?"

"I guess it's the stubborn streak I inherited from my mother. When someone tells me I can't make a go of it, I invariably go out of my way to prove them wrong."

He laughed out loud. "Then I'm glad I could help. By the way," He pointed to his plate of food with his fork. "This chili is excellent."

"I made it especially hot."

"I noticed. Then you remembered what I said?"

Feeling like a teenager on her first date, she lowered her gaze from his. "Of course. Something about cooling down."

The sexual tension between them had increased, but she wouldn't give in. She felt sure that if she gave Brad an inch, he'd take a mile. Breathing in deeply, she reminded herself that maturity and decorum was the way to go.

He reached across and took her hand in his. "I think we're gonna get along just fine together."

When she raised her eyes back to his, she could just see the glimmer of sexual promise. Then he handed her a sheet of folded paper. "I've had this legal document made up. It explains about the sale of the land in detail."

Cassie picked up a pen. "I'll sign it now."

With her pen poised over the document, he said, "Aren't you gonna read it?"

She shook her head. "No. I trust you. I know my uncle led you a merry race over it. I don't intend to stand in the way of your business."

"Cassie, you don't even know how much I'm offering."

"I'm sure it's plenty, Brad. Really." With a flourish, she signed the papers and handed the document back. "There, that's settled."

"Then thank you, Cassie. This means a great deal to me."

"You're welcome. I'm only sorry it took this long. I've spoken to several people, and they all said the same thing. Uncle Seth completely lost the plot after Vietnam. He was only twenty-four when he came back, but he became a total recluse and was clearly mentally unstable. As soon as I walked in here for the first time, I knew by the state of the place that he hadn't been playing with a full deck. Some of the things he must have witnessed in that awful war would have constantly been in his thoughts, even though it had been forty years since he was there."

"Yes, war can do strange things to the mind."

She began clearing the plates. "Would you like dessert, Brad? I have some ice cream."

He smiled, the creases forming as he stared directly into her eyes. "Yes, I'll have dessert, but I'll have mine later, much later."

He both unnerved her and excited her at the same time. Her voice now grew husky as she spoke to him, "Take your drink into the living room, Brad. I'll join you in a moment."

* * * *

As Brad settled into the sofa, he listened to the sounds coming from the kitchen as Cassie cleared away the dinner. Funny how he noticed the little things. Just the sound of the cutlery and crockery clinking together reminded him of his childhood. How comforting that time had been. After he'd made a life on his own, he'd always remained single. Why complicate things? But he had to admit that knowing a woman was close by who found him irresistible had a certain appeal.

He swirled the bourbon around in his glass and stared at the fire. Maybe a little piece of heaven had moved next door to him. If he treated her right, they'd have the perfect relationship. No ties and no commitments. Just great sex. Perfect.

Well he'd look after her tonight. That was for sure. For over ten years he'd been after that piece of land, and now he had it. His business could develop the way he wanted. By way of a thank you, he owed her a sinful night of pure sex.

He looked up when she entered the room, and he patted the empty seat next to him. He could already feel his cock hardening in anticipation, but he would draw it out a bit longer. Keep her panting with expectation, then she wouldn't be able to resist. "Now tell me about your parents. Are they still alive?"

She shook her head. "No, are yours?"

He rested his arm along the backrest, and she snuggled into his chest. "Yep, they are. They live over by Deer Lodge. Same house I was born in, too."

"Really? That's nice continuity. My mother died about four years ago from cancer, and my father from a bad heart some fifteen years ago."

"So you were quite young then?"

"Mmm, about eleven when Dad died, I think. Made me grow up fast."

He wondered if this lack of stability in her life had made her feel uncertain about the future. Her parents dying, and now a divorce. He could certainly understand her reluctance to commit fully to another man.

"So where did you meet your husband?"

"In college. We were both doing a course in business studies. I thought I'd found my lifelong mate, but," she shrugged, and he glimpsed the bitterness and intense disappointment on her face. Then she continued, "He took everything. The house I'd worked so hard to pay for, and even Sebastian. I hate him most of all for that."

He wondered if Sebastian was her child, and he asked, "Who's Sebastian?"

"Oh, he was my dog. A Samoyed. He knew he was mine, and yet he took him just to spite me."

Brad thought the guy sounded like a total dick. "Why?"

"I guess my best friend wanted to take over my life. She seemed to be able to twist Aaron around her little finger. Whatever she asked for, he gave her."

He assured her. "Sounds like a very manipulative woman. I'm sure they'll be very unhappy together."

She giggled. "Do you think so? That would make me feel so much better, Brad."

"Dollar to a dime says he'll be calling you up saying he made a mistake."

"Well he won't be in the least welcome." From her tone and the way her shoulders stiffened, he guessed he wouldn't.

He began massaging her neck. "The asshole sounds like a total loser to me."

"You're right. Mmm, that's so nice." She moved her head from side to side, enjoying the caress of his fingertips, and then closed her eyes.

He smiled to himself and leaned in and kissed her lips, running his tongue over them until she opened her mouth and allowed him full access.

The sound of her breathing increased as he slid his tongue deep inside her mouth. When he ran his hand up under her blouse to her breasts, she let out a small whimper as he grazed his thumb over her responsive nipples. They were so sensitive that they hardened as soon as he touched them.

So much for making the evening last. All he wanted to do was take her to bed and fuck her. He trailed kisses from her cheek to her neck and whispered seductively against her ear, "Cassie, how about you and I head upstairs, and I'll show you my appreciation for that piece of land you just sold me?"

Chapter Seven

He insisted on collecting some ice from the kitchen and then carried her up the stairs. Showering kisses over her face with each stair tread that he climbed. There was something quite primitive and sexy about a man carrying her to bed. Cassie could already feel desire pooling in her panties as the bedroom door swung open and he laid her on the bed.

Sex with Brad was something else entirely. He certainly knew how to please a woman. He seemed so self-assured as he unbuttoned her blouse and then unzipped her leather jeans.

"These are sexy as hell," he murmured, peeling them from her legs. "You're lucky you've kept them on this long."

She giggled as he cast them aside along with her panties. She tugged at his shirt impatiently.

"Brad, I don't know how you do it, but I always seem to have fewer clothes on than you do."

He smiled, staring into her eyes, and then stroked her hair. "That's because I plan ahead." He leaned forward and pulled the glass of ice from the nightstand.

Cassie's whole body stiffened and she giggled nervously. "I don't want that ice anywhere near me, Brad."

"You have to trust me, Cassie. I'm just gonna show you that sometimes the most sensual of feelings can come from the simplest of sensations."

He popped an ice cube into his mouth and then returned the glass to the stand.

He stood and removed his shirt, the muscles on his torso clearly defined from the small bedside lamp. When he discarded the rest of his clothes, anticipation flooded her mind. He was everything she'd ever wanted. Tall, good-looking, and incredibly sexy. No man had ever come remotely close. Most of all, their relationship was built on sexual needs. Nothing more. They were just here to enjoy each other's company. As her gaze drifted over him, she knew she would enjoy his body time and again.

Her heart began hammering in her chest as he returned to the bed, and she wondered just how this ice would affect her. Surely he must have swallowed it by now.

When he kissed her lips, she gasped from the exquisite sensation. His lips were warm, but his tongue felt ice cold.

He explored her breasts with his hands, and then followed with his mouth. The warmth of his lips and the coolness of his tongue sent delicious pulses racing through her body. "That's so cold."

"Baby, we've only just started." He placed another ice cube into his mouth and smiled at her.

This time when he suckled on her breasts, a white heat seared into her. Her nipples stood erect as he circled them with his tongue. The tips glistened from his gentle and sensual caress. He smiled as she arched away from him.

"Brad, it's so cold."

He held on to her, trailing kisses down her abdomen and stomach until he lifted her legs to bend at the knees. He then spread her legs apart.

She protested, but it had no effect as he licked her entire slit with his ice-cold tongue.

A delicious wanton feeling tore into her body. With her legs bent at the knees and his hands holding her firmly in place, she could barely move.

The tightrope between pleasure and pain felt indistinct. She could not fully comprehend either. The sensual touch of his mouth as he lapped at her clit did delightful things to her body. The freezing temperature of his tongue seemed so cold that it almost burned her sensitive flesh. The intensity of the moment made her hands fist tightly into his hair.

"Brad, oh, Brad."

Suckling on her clit, he licked and stroked until she thought she would die of the delicious erotic sensations.

"Brad," she cried out. "Oh, Brad." A scream tore from her lips as he finally drove his ice-cold tongue deep inside her sensitized pussy. The combination of heat and ice intensified her orgasm as it rippled and pulsed throughout her body.

Her whole being convulsed and she arched as it finally receded, collapsing back onto the bed. Her chest heaved as she fought to regain her breath.

* * * *

"Come here, baby," he murmured gruffly as he pulled her on top of him. He brushed the hair from her eyes and smiled as she finally managed to focus on him. She'd sure had one powerful orgasm. "Now you're gonna enjoy my heat like never before."

He maneuvered her so his cock lay poised at her moist entrance. "Is this what you want, baby?" He pushed inside her just enough, and she squirmed, wanting more. He gripped her more tightly, stopping her.

"Brad," she whimpered. "I need you." Her lips pouted. He hardly knew her, but his heart twisted in his gut. She needed him. A lot of women had said those very words to him during sex before, but somehow coming from Cassie the words made him feel extra special. Her moans spurred him on, and he watched her face as he slowly sunk inside her. Her eyelids drooped, and she leaned in and kissed his lips. "You feel so good, Brad."

Cassie responded to him on a different level to all the other women he'd known. She enjoyed sex the same way he did. It felt more intimate and satisfying. With her pussy sheathing his hard cock in a tight embrace, he began thrusting inside her.

"You like that?"

"Yes, Brad."

"And that?" He thrust harder.

"Oh, harder." She braced her hands against his chest as she raised herself upright, her body moving in tight circles around his cock. He watched her lose herself in the intense pleasure. Her hands smoothed over her own breasts, tweaking her nipples until they were pulled taut. When she leaned back and threaded her fingers into her hair, he thought she was the most beautiful woman he'd ever seen.

The sight of his thick dick glistening with her feminine juices and disappearing repeatedly into her wanton body brought him to the very peak of orgasm. He wouldn't be able to hold out much longer, but he'd try, if only to watch Cassie erupt into orgasm once again.

Bracing her hands on his thighs behind her, she arched back. "Oh, Brad." Her climax tightened around him, and he heard her cry out. Her body convulsing and milking his cock until he, too, finally gave in to instinct and spilled his warm cum deep inside her.

* * * *

"Mmm, this is lovely," she said, snuggling closer into his embrace. Her whole body felt relaxed and spent.

Brad kissed her forehead and pulled her closer. "You seemed totally absorbed in our love making."

Her fingers traced down his chest, smoothing into the hair. It felt soft to the touch and still glistened with beads of sweat from his exertions. "I'm sorry if I got carried away."

Brad let out a long, slow breath. He touched her cheek and angled her face to his. Looking into her eyes, he murmured, "Baby, you were everything a woman should be, and everything a man could ever want. You're like a fantasy made real."

Cassie giggled. "Fantasy, huh? I like that. What other fantasies do you have, Brad? I must say I really enjoyed the ice-cube. I was so glad for your warm cock afterward."

"That was the idea. I have plenty of fantasies, Cassie. I'm sure you know that already." Staring at her mouth, he kissed her and then traced his thumb over her lips. When he raised his gaze to hers, she saw a burning promise in his eyes. In time, she was sure he'd reveal them all. Then he asked, "Tell me your favorite fantasy, Cassie? I'd love to know."

"Oh, I don't have any." She lied.

"Uh-uh, don't give me that. All women have fantasies."

Her fingers drifted over his chest again. "You know me too well, Brad. Of course I have fantasies. It's just embarrassing to share them, that's all."

He stroked his hand into her hair, pulling a stray strand from the corner of her mouth. "I'm waiting."

She bit her fingernail. "Oh, this is so embarrassing, Brad."

"Go on."

"Well, it always starts in the middle of the night. I'm alone in the house, and I become aware that there's somebody outside. When I investigate, an intruder suddenly confronts me. He's good looking and says he's come to rob me, only he needs to tie me up while he ransacks the place, so I can't call the cops. Only, well, you know." She stopped talking, afraid to continue for fear of ridicule.

"No, I don't know. Go on," he urged. "You've got me interested now."

She shook her head. "It sounds ludicrous. Why would anyone fantasize over a stranger?"

"It's quite common, Cassie. It's all about giving control to someone else and letting them be responsible for your sexual desires. It frees you from the guilt of just pure sex." He smiled. "So go on."

"I can't believe I've told you that much. I have no intention of telling you anymore."

"Are you sure?"

"I am." She playfully swiped at his hand. "Talk about something else."

"Like what?"

"What you do in the mountains? Why you choose to take the difficult routes across them?"

"I usually take a group of three or four hardened riders. We head out for a couple of days, getting right off the beaten track. That's what most people come for. They want to feel as though they're exploring it for the first time. I guess I play into that dream."

"It does sound exciting, Brad. Do you sleep out under the stars?"

"Whenever possible. It can get cold at night, whatever the time of year, so there are tents, but I usually just hunker down into my sleeping bag and stare at the heavens above."

The more she heard, the more she realized Brad was a deep thinker. "Tell me about the stars, Brad? Do they shine brighter the higher you go?"

"They sure do, and the shooting stars are more prolific, too. When the skies are clear, you can get a terrific light show. I can name you every constellation. Cassiopeia, Ursa Major and Minor—"

"Okay, okay, I get the picture. You love being close to nature."

The way he spoke, she knew he had a real passion for the mountains. The local name for him, The Mountain Man, seemed very appropriate. Truth be told, she would love to go with him and see the sights for herself, but he didn't mention it, not even in passing, and she would never ask. Perhaps he wanted to keep that part of himself separate from her.

Well, she couldn't blame him for that. There were parts of her own life that she never wanted to share with anyone.

Chapter Eight

Christmas came and went, and although a low-key event, she'd enjoyed it all the same. It had been just the two of them, pleased to be in each other's company.

Brad had asked her if she wanted to go with him to meet his parents, but she'd declined, preferring her own company. Besides, his parents would only get the wrong idea about her. She and Brad were just good friends, although she knew she was becoming more attached to him than she cared to admit.

On Christmas Eve, he called for her with a team of four horses pulling a sleigh. It was so romantic, snuggling beneath a red and black checkered blanket as he took her for a sleigh ride along the valley. When they arrived back at his ranch, soft, golden light spilled onto the snow that had drifted around the walls of his home. Inside, a huge roaring log fire greeted her, along with a Christmas tree decorated with tinsel and baubles. She guessed Brad wanted it to be a Christmas to remember.

It was.

In the morning they exchanged gifts. She'd bought him a Breitling navigator's watch, and he'd bought her a new lacy set of expensive underwear to make up for the ones he'd ruined when he'd saved her life. The idea that Brad had gone into a sexy lingerie shop and picked them out especially for her, gave her a warm glow inside. Of course he'd insisted on her modeling them for him as soon as they were unwrapped. After parading around the room a couple of times in the red lace panties and bra, he'd wanted them off pretty quickly. He'd made love to her then, in front of the roaring log fire. It had been the best Christmas she'd ever had.

When the snows began to melt, her impatience grew for the warm mild air and the long summer nights. Coming to Montana had been the best thing she'd ever done.

Monday and Friday nights belonged to her and Brad. She would often catch herself running to the window when it was his turn to visit. The smile he gave her, always full of promise. Realization began to slowly dawn on her. She'd fallen for him in a big way.

As the days grew warmer, he'd ride over to her place on Rufus, looking every inch the Mountain Man in his tight jeans and black cowboy hat. They'd often laugh that Rufus looked none too pleased, sharing the night with her chickens in the barn.

With Brad often out trekking in the mountains, sometimes they wouldn't see each other for almost a week.

Early one June, while she was busy washing her Jeep, the sound of her cell phone brought her indoors.

"Hi, sugar."

Her heart leapt into her mouth, and she placed her hand on her chest in order to still it. "What do you want, Aaron?"

"I just thought I'd call to see how you are."

"Why?"

"Why not?"

This was so unlike him. It had been almost a year since their divorce. Instinctively she knew why he'd called. "Candy's left you, hasn't she?"

"Took me a while to realize I'd made a mistake, honey bun. I think losing our baby unsettled our relationship. Don't you?"

"Don't give me that, Aaron. You walked out when I needed you most. How dare you make that excuse."

Her hand shook, and she wiped the tears from her eyes. Why had he called her now? Just when she'd finally managed to leave all the hurt behind.

"Look, give me your address and I can come over and talk to you properly. I realize I've behaved badly, but we really had something special together."

"No, we didn't, Aaron. You never really loved me. That's why you left me for Candy. I don't want to see you ever again. Besides, I've met someone else."

His silence said it all. So he hadn't expected her to find anyone so soon. Then he asked, *"Does he love you?"*

Hesitating only momentarily, she said, "Of course." Brad had never uttered the word *love* at any time, but she wouldn't give her ex the satisfaction of knowing that.

"Honey bun, you're talking to me. Don't lie."

Her hand shook as she said coolly, "Aaron, you made your decision, now live with it. You're history, buddy. Don't contact me again." Then she disconnected the call and turned her cell phone off, making a mental note to change her number. Why hadn't she done that before? Had she secretly wanted him to call her?

Tears began to pour down her face. Now her love for Aaron had turned to hate. The fact that he'd used her miscarriage as an excuse for the breakup of their marriage only underlined the fact. How dare he?

Her mind drifted to Brad. He was more of a man than Aaron could ever be. Only he didn't love her. No matter how long their relationship lasted, he would never settle down. Aaron had immediately sensed that from the tone of her voice.

Staying with Brad would only lead to more heartache. He'd also made it clear that to broach the subject would only lead to the end of their relationship.

Feeling that she was between a rock and a hard place, there was only one decision she could make.

* * * *

When Cassie didn't arrive at her usual time, Brad went outside and looked up the valley. He was unsure if she'd already left, so he decided to call her number.

No answer.

Wondering if it was a repeat of the time she had the accident, he waited another five minutes and then decided to drive over there. Better to be safe than sorry.

When he arrived, he noticed that her Jeep was parked in the drive. He knocked on the door. Still no answer. Worried that she may be in trouble, he called out, "Cassie, open the door."

After a few moments, he heard her approach, and she let him in.

Her face looked all puffy from crying, and she averted her gaze from his. "What's wrong, Cassie? I was worried about you."

She shook her head and immediately burst into tears.

He held her in his arms then, and she sobbed against his T-shirt, making it wet. Whatever had upset her was clearly playing on her mind.

"What happened? Tell me." He sat her in the living room and joined her on the sofa, holding her close.

"My ex called."

Brad immediately felt himself stiffen. The guy was a prize asshole, and whatever he'd had to say had obviously upset her, but what he hated the most was another man had shown interest in Cassie. He didn't like it one little bit. In fact, it made him jealous as hell. If the dick head were here, he'd deck him without a second thought.

"Go on," he urged. "He said something, he must have done, or you wouldn't be so upset."

Fighting for composure, she breathed in. "A while back, I was having a baby. I miscarried, and Aaron now blames the emotional trauma on the breakup of our marriage. He said he'd made a mistake. He said he wants me back."

The blood pounded in his ears as rage began to overwhelm him. This was the worst thing possible. He didn't want Cassie to go back to

Minneapolis. *Why, Brad, why? Use your brain, cowboy, instead of your dick.*

Calmly, he said, "Is that what you want? Is that why you're upset?" *Why don't you just tell her how you feel?* He had fallen in love with her, but he was just too stubborn and macho to tell her. He knew she'd become attached to him, too. Yet, he refused to tell her how much he loved her. Just how much of an uncaring bastard was he?

Cassie just stared at him for a moment, and then she started to cry even more. Deep, heart-wrenching sobs that shook her whole body. He stroked her hair until she'd composed herself.

"Brad, you don't understand, I hate him."

He felt relief, but she began to pull away from him. "He hurt me, and I'm scared of being hurt all over again.

So that was it. Here it was. The ultimatum. *It's me or nothing.* Only this time he didn't want to choose nothing.

"Cassie, baby." He pulled her back into his arms. "Let's not make a decision now. Let's think on it. When we're calm, we can do it properly." He needed time to think more clearly. He didn't want to make a snap decision either way.

He stroked her hair. "You've had a hard time, what with the divorce and losing a baby. It must have been very difficult."

"It was. That's why I moved all the way out here to Whitewaters. I've really enjoyed these last few months, only he just spoiled it. I should have changed my number." She rested her head against his shoulder, and briefly closed her eyes.

"Feeling better?" he asked as her breathing started to return to normal.

She nodded. "Yes, Brad, thank you." She looked sad as she stared at him, and he guessed she thought their relationship was over, too.

"Is there anything you want me to do? Would you like a glass of water? Anything?"

"Just hold me, Brad. I just need to feel you close to me." He realized he needed that, too, and he pulled her into his arms. They were just a whisker away from finishing their relationship. Now he had some important thinking to do. At thirty-five, wasn't it time he took life a little more seriously?

* * * *

Standing at her bedroom window, Cassie looked at the full moon rising above the mountains on the far side of the valley. If she stared long enough, she could just make out the different crags and gullies.

Unable to sleep, she wondered if Brad was amongst their peaks. Since that day, five days ago, when she'd become upset, she hadn't heard from him.

Admittedly, he had calmed her down, but she felt as though she'd pushed him into a corner by giving him an ultimatum. It had been a dreadful day, first that awful phone call from Aaron and then the gut wrenching thought that the relationship she shared with Brad was over. At least he'd stopped her from making a decision there and then. Surely she should take some small comfort from that.

Knowing Brad so well now, she assumed he was just saving her inevitable rejection until a more suitable time. Otherwise, he would have told her he loved her, or at least told her he cared for her.

Pacing the bedroom floor once more, she decided to go downstairs and watch a late-night movie. Something to help get her through the night and take her mind off things.

Cassie settled into the sofa, and switched on the TV. After flicking through the channels, she eventually decided on a horror movie.

After clasping her knees to her chest, she pulled her pale blue silk gown around herself, and stared at the screen. Maybe a horror movie was not such a good idea after all. She wished Brad were here. She always felt so safe when he was around.

When the lights suddenly went out, a short, sharp squeal left her lips. Admonishing herself for being so ridiculously childish, she gathered herself together. A storm had knocked out the power lines two days before, and she silently cursed the generator. Now she would have to go outside and try to restart the brute.

Taking the flashlight from the kitchen drawer, she took some comfort from the solid beam of light. If she couldn't restart the generator, she'd leave it until morning when daylight returned.

Once outside, Cassie opened the annex door where the generator was housed. The strong beam of light picked out the mess inside. The whole place needed a complete clear out. All of Uncle Seth's old furniture had been dumped in there. It rose high off the floor, stacks of chairs and old bedsteads, pine dressers, and old wicker tables.

As she walked over to the generator, she heard something move behind her. Turning around, she shone the beam of light in the direction of the noise.

The sound came again, only its position had changed, and she quickly turned the flashlight in the new direction. "Is someone there?" she said, her voice more shaky than she would have liked. She had the sinking feeling that she was not alone. Her heart began beating faster, and a cold, clammy feeling washed over her. If that was the case, what was she going to do?

The sound of metal running along the railings of the old bed frame in the corner of the annex sent her whirling in that direction.

"I have a gun," she lied. "If you come any closer, I'll shoot."

Her heart lurched, banging against her ribs. She had never felt so frightened and vulnerable in her life. Miles from anywhere, there would be no help.

Fear gripped her body, paralyzing her movements. There was only one small glimmer of hope.

"Brad, tell me it's you." Her hands began shaking, and the beam of light wavered in front of her. "Please, tell me it's you, Brad." Her tone was almost pleading.

Just when she thought panic would overwhelm her, a deep, seductive voice filtered through the air. "You got the wrong guy, lady."

Her throat went dry with fear, and her voice sounded strangled and frightened. "Oh my God, please don't hurt me, please don't hurt me."

"You got that right, lady. You do what I tell you, when I tell you. You understand? See things my way, and I might let you live."

Her hands shook so much the torch fell from her grasp and dropped to the floor, plunging them into total darkness. She was so frightened, and yet so excited, too.

Brad had returned as her fantasy man.

"Please tell me what you want. I'll do whatever you say." Her breathy words pierced the total darkness.

"That's right, lady. You will do exactly what I want. If you scream, there'll be trouble. Do you understand?"

"Yes." Her voice was now barely a whisper.

"Put your hands behind your back. I'm gonna tie you up."

Suddenly the fantasy was about to become reality. Deep down, she knew that Brad would never hurt her, but if she did as he asked, she would have to have complete trust in him. Brad had shown her many things in the last six months. Most of all, he'd taught her how to enjoy life again. This would be just part of getting to know herself as a woman, and believing in Brad as a man.

Slowly she placed her hands behind her back and awaited her fate. A primitive gasp escaped her lips as he bound her wrists tightly together. Her whole body shook from the contact.

"Good girl," he murmured as he tightened the knot.

Testing the bindings she realized that though they didn't hurt her, they would not give.

It was only then that he moved in front of her. In the darkness, she could barely see him, just the faint glint of his eyes twinkling in the soft moonlight that streamed through the open doorway. Desire flared instantly. To be at his mercy simply turned her on. She felt sexy as hell, and her breasts heaved in anticipation of things to come.

"Now you're coming with me," he announced gruffly as he hauled her effortlessly onto his shoulder and began carrying her inside the house.

Chapter Nine

For a brief moment, he thought Cassie would chicken out. He just caught the small delay when he'd ordered her to put her arms behind her back. She knew what that meant. He guessed she'd been weighing up the consequences.

Admittedly he'd surprised her, but that had been part of the plan. What better way to show her who he really was? A risk taker, he'd decided to make her fantasy come true. Her whole body had vibrated in anticipation and fear as he'd bound her wrists, and he knew it turned her on. The idea of controlling her sure turned him on, too. He felt horny as fuck. The hard-on in his jeans clear evidence of that.

Deliberately cutting the power had been a good way to set the fantasy in motion. It only added to the excitement.

As he carried her up the stairs, he felt her heart beating fast against his body. He guessed her pussy would already be wet.

"Please let me go. I promise I won't call the cops."

"You got that right, lady. Ain't nobody coming to help you. It's just you and me. Besides, I've cut the phone lines."

"Please, tell me what you want." Her breathing had become labored.

"Baby, you and I are gonna have some real good fun together, and then when I'm done, you're gonna give me all your money. Do you understand?"

"Yes."

Cassie was really into the role now, and he could feel her struggling on his shoulder. "Quit twisting, lady. You're only making it worse for yourself."

He kicked the bedroom door open with a booted foot and tipped her bound body onto the bed. Lying on her back, she tried to move, but with her arms tied behind her, she found it almost impossible. Now this was going to be enjoyable.

He began shedding his clothes. In the silver moonlight streaming through the bedroom window, he could just make out the outline of her body in her silk gown, her blonde hair cascading over her shoulders.

Her eyes on his, watching and waiting to see what he would do next. The rapid rise and fall of her chest, a clear indication of her sexual arousal. Cassie was as turned on as he was. If he could just draw the fantasy out, it sure would be a night to remember.

* * * *

When the bed creaked, she knew he would do whatever he wanted. Anticipation whipped through her body like never before.

A small gasp left her lips as he pulled her into a kneeling position and came up close behind her.

"Now if you scream, I'll make it worse for you. Do you understand?"

Swallowing, she nodded. Brad sounded different. He was taking this fantasy seriously. There was not a hint of play acting in his demeanor. This only heightened her awareness of him as he pressed his large frame against her back. The warmth of his body permeated her flimsy silk gown. Her whole body shook with sexual excitement, and she knew he would be aware of that, too.

"This needs to come off, lady." He yanked at her gown. The material tore noisily in the deathly quiet of the bedroom. With several successive sharp pulls, he ripped it completely from her, exposing her flesh to the cool night air. Feeling out of control, her body vibrated from his caveman-style actions. Desire pooled in her pussy, making her wet and ready for his huge dick that pressed deliciously against her bound hands.

"Now, I'm gonna enjoy this." His warm breath rasped against her neck.

"Please don't."

"Ain't no use begging, lady. I'm gonna fuck you good and proper."

His hands began to explore her body. Starting at her neck and drifting lower to cup both her breasts. He massaged them in tight, concentric circles, feeling their generous weight as he lifted them in his hands.

The combination of her fantasy and the experienced movement of his touch against her skin made her gasp. It didn't feel like Brad at all. It actually felt like a stranger fondling her breasts. Her body arched from the contact, and she moaned with pleasure.

"See, there's nothing you can do, is there?"

The hard ridge of his cock pushed against her bound hands, the pressure of his weight emphasizing the restraints on her wrists.

"Feel that? My dicks so fucking hard," he whispered against her ear. "Soon that's gonna be inside you." His one hand slipped lower, caressing her abdomen. His tongue tasted her spine and she arched away from the exquisite feeling, the bindings on her wrists both exciting her and restricting her movements.

The fingers of his one hand brushed against her pussy. "Open your legs."

"Please don't make me," she panted. She shook her head, knowing that resistance was futile. He was dominant, no question.

"I won't ask you again, lady, or I'll do it for you."

She couldn't have responded quickly enough because he pushed her head down toward the mattress and forcibly spread her legs with his knees from behind. "You've disobeyed me. I'll have to punish you," he murmured gruffly, thrusting his hand along her slit and penetrating her wet pussy with his fingers. This felt so forbidden and erotic. With her hands tied behind her back in a submissive posture, her face was pushed further into the mattress. Cassie felt totally at his mercy.

Without warning, he slapped her ass hard with his other hand. The stinging sensation only heightened the feel of his fingers deep inside her pussy. He did it again, and her inner muscles clamped down on him even harder.

"Oh, God," her whimper of submission, as he continued to stroke and spank her.

"Have you learned your lesson?"

"Yes."

"You call me Master."

"I'm sorry. Yes, Master."

"Will you ever disobey me again?"

"No, Master."

He gave her one last hard slap on her ass. "Okay, now you're ready for me."

* * * *

He flipped her onto her back. She looked so fucking sexy, her body arched because her hands were bound behind her. Her pussy raised up and just begging to be fucked.

He cupped her chin and leaned in to taste her lips. His tongue delving inside her mouth. "You're mine to do with as I please. Say it." His breathing had increased in anticipation. His cock stood to attention, the moist tip of his bell end glistening with pre-cum, rested against his taut stomach.

Her baby blue eyes blinked at him, and she licked her parched lips. "I'm yours, Master, to do with as you see fit. Please untie me. I promise I won't run."

"No, not until I'm ready. You look so fucking sexy, I want to take you like this."

Still in a kneeling position, he pulled her toward him. Her legs lay across his thighs, defining the arch of her body even more. When his hard cock rested at her entrance, he spoke, "You want me to fuck you like this, don't you?"

"Yes, Master."

"You like me in control, don't you?"

"Yes, Master."

He slid his shaft slowly inside her. The fact that she was still bound at the wrists only heightened his arousal. The incredible moans she made as he sunk his cock deep inside her blew his mind.

Her whole body arched in front of him, so beautiful as if carved from marble. Her full, creamy breasts thrust out, inviting him. The tips peaked and aroused. The diamond jewelry at her navel glinted from the subdued moonlight. It rose in time with her out-of-control breathing.

Holding her hips to steady himself, he began thrusting his length inside her. The angle was just perfect to stimulate her G-spot. Each stroke of his cock made her moan out loud, tight whimpers that urged him on, faster and faster.

When she cried out, "Oh, my God," he knew she was close, and he slowed the tempo down, drawing it out as he leaned in and covered her body with his. Bracing his hands either side of her head, he held his weight from her.

He kissed her lips and she responded, feverishly kissing him back. He wanted to experience everything about her. Trailing kisses down her neck, he ran his tongue to her breasts, lapping at the pale pink peaks, over and over until she arched under him, offering them to his hungry mouth. He suckled on the hardened nubs as he drove his cock repeatedly inside her. Their stomachs touching as he ground himself into her time and again. Sweat glistened where their bodies met.

Her moist, velvet sheath tightened around him as her climax became inevitable and reached the point of no return. Holding a hand under her ass, he thrust harder.

"Come for me, Cassie," he whispered against her ear, running his tongue against her soft delicate skin. Tasting her exquisite essence.

Her feminine whimpers spurred him on, and as her orgasm shattered and convulsed around his thick length, a powerful force surged up his shaft. The feeling was so intense as his cum pumped inside her that a deep-throated growl left his lips. His spent body lay across hers. The sweat from their exertions mixing, their bodies and minds joined.

Sex with Cassie had always been great, but this had been mind blowing.

* * * *

As she fought for breath, Brad rolled her onto her stomach and began to untie her hands. "Come here," he said, pulling her into his arms when he'd finally freed her from the restraints.

"That felt amazing, Brad." Her whole body tingled from the exhilaration of it all. She loved Brad with all her heart. There could be no one else in her life. No other man could ever come close to how she felt about him.

He laughed. "I took a chance that you'd go along with it. I hope I didn't scare you too much."

She couldn't deny she'd been scared, but so very excited, too. "Those few minutes when I didn't know it was you were just awful. You should have warned me."

He wrapped her more tightly in his arms. "I'm sorry, baby. Guess I thought it would make it an experience to remember."

"Well you certainly did that. I'm definitely going to get me a guard dog now. It just showed me how vulnerable I really am, living on my own."

He stroked his hand through her hair, and she snuggled into his warmth. "Perhaps you won't always be on your own, Cassie." He opened his mouth, and then closed it again. "Look, Cassie, the reason

I came over this late was to take you for a midnight ride. I guess I kinda got distracted."

She giggled. "Mmm, well you certainly distracted me, too."

"Mmm, I noticed." He kissed her slowly, a smile forming as he looked intently at her, the lines at the side of his mouth deepening in that sexy way she loved so much. "Come on, let's get dressed. There's a beautiful moon tonight, and I think you'll enjoy it."

* * * *

Brad helped her onto Rufus, and then he eased himself behind her. As he took the reins with one hand, he circled her waist with the other. The whole of his warm body cradled her from his broad chest to his powerful thighs.

He breathed in deeply. "You smell so feminine," he murmured against her hair as he began guiding Rufus down the well-worn track. "My, this feels good."

"Mmm, it sure does." Cassie thought it felt like heaven. The fact that Brad had invited her on a ride at all made her heart swell. It showed that he wanted to share that part of his life, too. Though she had to remind herself that this was just a ride, albeit at midnight.

"Where are we going?" she eventually asked as they crossed the part of the river that now belonged to him.

"It's only another half hour or so. There's a good vantage point. Thought you might like to sleep under the stars with me tonight."

To Cassie, it sounded like the most romantic thing she'd ever heard. She ran her hand over his, reveling in his masculine warmth. "I couldn't think of anything I'd rather do, Brad."

"Good, that's exactly what I wanted to hear."

"Rufus seems to be very sure-footed," Cassie remarked after he'd negotiated what seemed to her an impossible ridge.

"Oh, he's a smart horse. Knows the route and takes his time. He may not be fast, but he's safe."

Patting the horse's neck, she laughed. "Take no notice of your master, Rufus. I think you're plenty fast enough."

Eventually, they reached a plateau and the ground leveled out. Brad dismounted and helped her from Rufus. His strong, masculine arms making her feel safe and protected. She slid into his embrace, and he kissed her slowly. His hands gently cupping her face as he smiled down at her.

"Baby, you sure look beautiful tonight."

"Must be the moonlight." He took her hand in his, and they both became silent for a few seconds as they admired the panoramic view. The whole valley spread out below them in eerie silence. The beautiful full moon gave them just enough light to see by. He put his arm around her shoulders as they took in the surreal, dreamlike scene.

"So many stars, Brad." They twinkled brightly, and she gazed in awe at how many filled the night sky. She gasped when she saw a shooting star, followed almost immediately by another one, arcing brightly across the night sky before fading away entirely.

"If you see a shooting star, you have to make a wish," he announced.

Cassie closed her eyes, knowing her wish stood right beside her.

"What did you wish for?" he asked when she opened her eyes.

She shook her head. "Oh, no. If I tell you, it'll never come true."

"Then I'll tell you mine." He pulled her into his arms. "I've fallen in love with you, Cassie. I'm thirty-five, and I want to commit to you. We're so alike. I want to spend the rest of my life with you. If you marry me, you'll make me the happiest man alive." His lips covered hers in a possessive embrace.

Surely, this was the most wonderful thing to have ever happened to her. Brad loved her. All fear and indecision left her body. Everything about the past seemed to be of no significance now. She doubted she'd ever give a second thought to Aaron ever again. With this man of hers, she could take on the world. Whatever life threw at them, she knew they would overcome.

Flinging her arms around his neck, she pulled him toward her. "My answer, Brad, is yes, yes, yes. I didn't think I could ever love again, but you've taught me how to trust once more. I love you with all my heart and I don't want to go through this life without you. You've made me the happiest woman alive. You've made my wish come true."

Epilogue

Two years later

Cassie smiled and waved at Brad as he turned Rufus loose into the paddock. The horse kicked and bucked, enjoying the freedom as he romped around the enclosure.

Brad strode quickly toward her, and she ran into his arms. For five long days and nights, she'd have him all to herself before he took another expedition back into the mountains.

He gathered her up and spun her around.

"Did you miss me, baby, because I sure missed you."

"You know I did." It had been three days since she'd seen him last.

He kissed her lips, a promise of things to come.

"How's junior?" he asked as they strolled hand in hand into the ranch house.

"He's almost talking. I'm sure he said Daddy earlier today."

"Wow, who's a clever boy," Brad cooed, as he lifted Donovan from the high chair in the kitchen. He bounced him in his arms, making their son chuckle with delight.

As she watched them both, Cassie knew she had found a little piece of heaven right here on earth. She had a family all her own to love and to cherish. She walked up to Brad and kissed him on his cheek.

"I love you."

He put an arm around her waist and hugged her close. "I love you, too, Cassie, and I always will."

In contentment, she breathed in his scent. He smelled of campfires, and the wind and the rain. He evoked everything she adored about Montana. He was her Montana Mountain Man, and she loved him…forever and ever.

THE END

www.janbowles.com

ABOUT THE AUTHOR

At present Jan Bowles lives with her husband in an old farmhouse in Lincolnshire, England, UK.

She would like to think that she's a free spirit, having lived in various parts of the UK and Europe. When she was younger she lived in Los Angeles, and travelled by car across the entire length of Route 66 to Chicago and then finally linked the journey to New York. It was an experience that Jan has never forgotten.

Jan has an enquiring mind, and will often muse about events having an everlasting effect on the human psyche. There is always a reason why people act the way they do. You just have to look below the surface. She hopes to bring these ideas to her writing.

When she's not writing Jan likes to paint large landscapes and sweeping vistas. She loves walking, and there's nothing more she'd rather do, than stand on the top of a hill with the wind blowing through her hair, and yep, if it's raining that's all the better. Jan says there's nothing like nature to make one feel truly alive.

Also by Jan Bowles

Siren Classic: *Dark Secrets*
BookStrand Mainstream: *The Return*
BookStrand Mainstream: *Love Lessons with the Texas Billionaire*
Siren Classic: Guilty Pleasures 1: *In Debt to the Dom*
Everlasting Classic: Guilty Pleasures 2: *Bought for the Billionaire's Bed*
Siren Classic: The Cowboy Mavericks: *Roped*

Available at
BOOKSTRAND.COM

Siren Publishing, Inc.
www.SirenPublishing.com